DEATH ON GIBRALTAR

SAS
OPERATION

Death on Gibraltar

SHAUN CLARKE

HARPER

This novel is entirely a work of fiction based on a factual event. The real names of the three IRA terrorists shot dead on Gibraltar on 8 March 1988 have been retained, as have those of the eight IRA men killed at Loughgall, Northern Ireland, on 8 May the previous year. Many events are partially or wholly the work of the author's imagination; all other names, characters and incidents portrayed in it are wholly the work of the author's imagination. Any resemblance to other actual persons, living or dead, events or localities is entirely coincidental.

Harper
An imprint of HarperCollins*Publishers*
1 London Bridge Street,
London SE1 9GF
www.harpercollins.co.uk

This paperback edition 2016
1

First published by 22 Books/Bloomsbury Publishing plc 1994

Copyright © Bloomsbury Publishing plc 1994

Shaun Clarke asserts the moral right to
be identified as the author of this work

A catalogue record for this book
is available from the British Library

ISBN: 978 0 00 815530 8

Set in Sabon by Born Group using Atomik ePublisher from Easypress

Printed and bound in Great Britain

MIX
Paper from
responsible sources
FSC
www.fsc.org **FSC™ C007454**

FSC is a non-profit international organisation established
to promote the responsible management of the world's forests.
Products carrying the FSC label are independently certified
to assure consumers that they come from forests that are managed
to meet the social, economic and ecological needs
of present and future generations.

Find out more about HarperCollins and the environment at
www.harpercollins.co.uk/green

Prelude

On the evening of Thursday 7 May 1987 fifteen soldiers from G Squadron, SAS, all dressed in standard DPM windproof, tight-weave cotton trousers and olive-green cotton battle smocks with British Army boots and maroon berets, were driven in four-wheel-drive Bedford lorries from their base at Stirling Lines, Hereford, to RAF Brize Norton, Oxfordshire, where they boarded a Hercules C-130 transport plane.

The men were armed with L7A2 7.62mm general-purpose machine-guns (GPMGs), 7.62mm Heckler & Koch G3-A4K twenty-round assault rifles with LE1-100 laser sights, and 5.56mm M16 thirty-round Armalite rifles. They also had many attachments for the various weapons, including bipods, telescopic sights, night-vision aids, and M203 40mm grenade-launchers. The ubiquitous standard-issue 9mm Browning High Power handgun was holstered at each man's hip. Their personal kit, including ammunition, water, rations, a medical pack, and spare clothing and batteries, was packed in the square-frame Cyclops bergens on their backs. Finally, they had with them crates filled with various items of high-tech communications and surveillance equipment, including Nikon F-801 35mm SLR cameras with Davies Minimodulux hand-held image intensifiers for night photography, a PRC319 microprocessor-based tactical radio, Pace Communications Ltd Landmaster III hand-held transceivers and Radio Systems Inc. walkie-talkies.

From RAF Brize Norton, the men were flown to RAF Aldergrove in Belfast, where they were transferred with their kit to three unmarked Avis vans and then driven through the rolling green countryside to the Security Forces base built around the old mill in the village of Bessbrook. There they were united with the twenty-four SAS men already serving in Northern Ireland, making a total force of thirty-nine specially trained and experienced counter-terrorist troopers.

The next morning was spent in a draughty lecture hall in the SF base where, with the aid of maps and a scale model of the Royal Ulster Constabulary police station of Loughgall, the combined body of men were given a final briefing on the operation to come.

Early that afternoon, when the RUC had thrown a discreet cordon around the area, diverting traffic and keeping all but local people out, the SAS men, with their weapons and surveillance equipment, were transported in the rented vans to Loughgall. Small and mostly Protestant, Loughgall is surrounded by the rolling green hills and apple trees of the 'orchard country' of north Armagh. It is some eight miles from Armagh city, and the road which leads from Armagh slopes down into the village, passing a walled copse on the right. The RUC station is almost opposite, between a row of bungalows, a former Ulster Defence Regiment barracks, the football team's clubhouse and a small telephone exchange. It is small enough to be run by a sergeant and three or four officers, and unimportant enough to be open only limited hours in the morning and afternoon, always closing completely at 7 p.m.

That day, well before the 'barracks', as the RUC station is known locally, was closed, some of the SAS men entered the building to occupy surveillance and firing positions at the rear and front, those at the front keeping well away from one particular side. While they were taking up positions inside, the rest were dividing into separate groups to set up ambushes around the building.

Two GPMG teams moved into the copse overlooking the police station, which enabled them to cover the football pitch facing it on the other side of the Armagh road. Others took up positions closer to and around the building, and behind the blast-proof wall protecting the front door.

Another team took the high ground overlooking the rear of the building. The remainder assumed positions in which they could act as cordon teams staking out the approach road in both directions.

Meanwhile, as members of the RUC's Headquarters Mobile Support Units were deployed in the vicinity, companies of UDR and British Army soldiers, as well as mobile police squads, were ready to cordon off the area after the operation.

That same afternoon a group of masked men hijacked a blue Toyota Hiace van at gunpoint from a business in Mountjoy Road, Dungannon. Sometime after five o'clock the same group hijacked a mechanical digger from a Dungannon farm, and the vehicle was driven to another farmyard about nine miles north of Loughgall.

With the SAS in position inside the RUC station, the building was locked up at the usual time. The troopers dug in around it had melted into the scenery, and apart from the sound of the wind, there was absolute silence.

* * *

Just before seven o'clock that evening, in the farmhouse north of Loughgall, close to the Armagh–Tyrone border and the Republican strongholds of Washing Bay and Coalisland, an IRA 'bucket bomb' team carefully loaded a 200lb bomb – designed to be set off by lighting a simple fuse – on to the bucket of the hijacked mechanical digger. Waiting close by, and watching them nervously, was a support team consisting of two Active Service Units of the East Tyrone Brigade of the IRA. Inside their stolen van was a collection of weapons that included three Heckler & Koch G3 7.62mm assault rifles, two 5.56mm FNC rifles, an assault shotgun and a German Ruger revolver taken from one of the reserve constables shot dead during a raid at Ballygawley eighteen months earlier.

Of the three-man bucket bomb team, one was a twenty-one-year-old with five years' IRA service, including several spells of detention; another had six years in the IRA behind him and had been arrested and interrogated many times because of it; and the third had twelve years' IRA service and six years' imprisonment.

The leader of one ASU team was thirty-year-old Patrick Kelly. Though known to be almost rigidly puritanical about his family and religious faith, Kelly was the commander of East Tyrone Provisional IRA units and suspected of murdering two RUC officers. The other ASU team was led by thirty-one-year-old Jim Lynagh, a former Sinn Fein councillor with fifteen years in the IRA and various terms in prison to his name. Though Lynagh, in direct contrast to Kelly, was an extrovert, good-humoured personality, he was suspected of many killings and, though acquitted of assassinating a UDR soldier, was widely believed to have done the deed.

The rest of the ASU teams consisted of a thirty-two-year-old escaper from the Maze Prison with fifteen years' violent IRA service to his credit; a nineteen-year-old who had been in the IRA for three years and claimed that he had been threatened with assassination by the RUC; and a twenty-five-year-old who had been in the IRA for five years, had been arrested many times and was a veteran of many terrorist operations.

These eight men were hoping to repeat the success of a similar attack they had carried out eighteen months earlier at Ballygawley, when they had shot their way into the police station, killing two officers, and then blown up the building.

This time, however, as they loaded their bomb on to the digger, they were being watched by a police undercover surveillance team, Special Branch's E4A, which was transmitting reports of their movements to the SAS men located in and around Loughgall RUC station.

The five armed men accompanying the three bombers had initially come along to ensure that no RUC men would escape through the back door of the building, as they had done at Ballygawley. However, just before climbing into their unmarked van, the two team leaders, Kelly and Lynagh, appeared – at least to the distant observers of E4A – to become embroiled in some kind of argument. Though what they said is not known, the argument was later taken by the Security Forces to be a sign of a last-minute confusion that could explain why, by the time the terrorists reached Loughgall in the stolen Toyota, their original plan for covering the back of the RUC police station had been dropped and they prepared to attack only the unguarded side of the building. Ironically, by ignoring the rear of the building, they were repeating the mistake they had made eighteen months earlier.

Their plan was to ignite the fuse on the bomb, then ram the RUC station with the bomb still in the bucket of the digger. They chose the side of the building because of the protection afforded the front entrance by the blast-proof wall. As an alternative to the usual attacks with heavy mortars or RPG7 rockets, this tactic had first been attempted eighteen months earlier at Ballygawley, then again, nine months later, at the Birches, Co. Tyrone, only five miles from Loughgall. Both operations had been successful.

To avoid the Security Forces, the terrorists travelled from the farmyard to Loughgall via the narrow, winding side lanes, rather than taking the main Dungannon-Armagh road. The five-man support team were in the blue van, driven by Seamus Donnelly, with one of the team leaders, Lynagh, in the back and Kelly in the front beside the driver. The van was in the lead to enable Kelly to check that the road ahead was clear. The mechanical digger followed, driven by Declan Arthurs and with Tony Gormley and Gerard O'Callaghan 'riding shotgun', though with their weapons concealed. The bucket bomb was hidden under a pile of rubble.

While the terrorists thought they were avoiding the Security Forces, their movements were almost certainly observed at various points along the route by surveillance teams in unmarked 'Q' cars or covert observation posts.

The Toyota van passed through Loughgall village at a quarter past seven. SAS men were hiding behind the wall of the church as it drove past them, but they held their fire. They wanted the van and mechanical digger to reach the police station as this would give the SAS men inside an excuse to open fire in 'self-defence'.

At precisely 7.20 p.m., possibly trying to ascertain if anyone was still in the building, Arthurs drove the mechanical digger to and fro a few times, with Gormley and O'Callaghan now deliberately putting their weapons on view. What happened next is still in dispute.

As the terrorists all knew that the Loughgall RUC station was empty from seven o'clock every evening, their timing of the attack is surely an indication that their purpose was to destroy the building, not take lives. More importantly, it begs the question of why the ASU team leader, Patrick Kelly, a very experienced and normally astute IRA fighter, would do what he is reported to have done.

Though believing that the police station was empty, Kelly climbed out of the cabin of the Toyota van with the driver, Donnelly, and proceeded to open fire with his assault rifle on the front of the building. Donnelly and some of the others then did the same.

Instantly, the SAS ambush party inside the building opened fire with a fearsome combination of 7.62mm Heckler & Koch G3-A4K assault rifles and 5.56mm M16 Armalites, catching the terrorists in a devastating fusillade, perforating the rear and side of the van with bullets and mowing down some of the men even before the 7.62mm GPMGs in the copse had roared into action, peppering the front of the van and catching the remaining terrorists in a deadly crossfire.

Hit several times, Kelly fell close to the cabin of the van with blood spreading out around him from a fatal head wound. Realizing what was happening, the experienced Jim Lynagh and Patrick McKearney scurried back into the van, but died in a hail of bullets that tore through its side panel. Donnelly had scrambled back into the driver's seat, but was mortally wounded in the same rain of bullets before he could move off. After ramming the mechanical digger into the side of the building, the driver, Arthurs, and another terrorist, Eugene Kelly, died as they tried in vain to take cover behind the bullet-riddled Toyota.

Even as the driver of the mechanical digger was dying in a hail of bullets, O'Callaghan was igniting the fuse of the

200lb bomb with a Zippo lighter. He then took cover beside Gormley.

The roar of the exploding bomb drowned out even the combined din of the GPMGs, assault rifles and Armalites. The spiralling dust and boiling smoke eventually settled down to reveal that the explosion had blown away most of the end of the RUC station nearest the gate, demolished the telephone exchange next door, and showered the football clubhouse with raining masonry. The mechanical digger had been blown to pieces and one of its wheels had flown about forty yards, to smash through a wooden fence and land on the football pitch. Some of the police and SAS men inside the building had been injured by the blast and flying debris.

When the bomb went off, Gormley and O'Callaghan tried to run for cover, but Gormley was cut down by heavy SAS gunfire as he emerged from behind the wall where he had taken cover. O'Callaghan was cut to pieces as he ran across the road from the badly damaged building.

But the IRA men were not the only casualties.

Because the GPMG teams hidden in the copse were targeting a building that stood close to the Armagh road, the oblique direction of fire meant that they also fired many rounds into the football pitch opposite and into parts of the village, including the wall of the church hall, where children were playing at the time. In addition, three civilian cars were passing between the RUC station and the church as the battle commenced.

Driving in a white Citroën past the church and down the hill towards the police station, Oliver Hughes, a thirty-six-year-old father of three, and his brother Anthony heard the thunderclap of the massive bomb, braked to a halt immediately and started to reverse the car. Unfortunately, both men were in overalls similar to those worn by the terrorists, so the SAS soldiers hidden near the church, assuming they were terrorist reinforcements, opened fire, peppering the Citroën with bullets, killing Oliver Hughes outright and badly wounding his brother, who took three rounds in the back and one in the head.

Travelling in the opposite direction, up the hill towards the church, another car, containing a woman and her young daughter, was also sprayed with bullets and screeched to a halt. In this instance, before anyone was killed the commander of one of the SAS groups raced through the hail of bullets to drag the woman and her daughter out of the car to safety. Miraculously, he succeeded.

The third car contained an elderly couple, Mr and Mrs Herbert Buckley. Both jumped out of their car and threw themselves to the ground, to survive unscathed.

Another motorist, a brewery salesman, had stopped his car even closer to the main action – between the IRA's Toyota and the copse where the two GPMG crews were dug in – and looked on in stunned disbelief as a rain of GPMG bullets hit the blue van. During a lull in the firing, he jumped out of his car and ran to find shelter behind the bungalows next to the police station. He never reached them, for after being rugby-tackled by an SAS trooper, he was held in custody until his identity could be established.

When the firing ceased, all eight of the IRA terrorists were found to be dead. Within thirty minutes, even as British Gazelle reconnaissance helicopters were flying over the area and British Army troops were combing the countryside in the vain pursuit of other terrorists, the SAS men were already being lifted out.

The deaths of the eight terrorists were the worst set-back the IRA had experienced in sixty years. During their funerals the IRA made it perfectly clear that bloody retaliation could be expected. It was a threat that could not be ignored by the British government.

1

'It is the belief of our Intelligence chiefs,' the man addressed only as 'Mr Secretary' informed the top-level crisis-management team in a basement office in Whitehall on 6 November 1987, 'that the successful SAS ambush in Loughgall last May, which resulted in the deaths of eight leading IRA terrorists, will lead to an act of reprisal that's probably being planned right now.'

There was a moment's silence while the men sitting around the boardroom table took in what the Secretary was saying so gravely. This particular crisis-management team was known as COBR – it represented the Cabinet Office Briefing Room – and all those present were of considerable authority and power in various areas of national defence and security. Finally, after a lengthy silence, one of them, a saturnine, grey-haired man from British Intelligence, said: 'If that's the case, Mr Secretary, we should place both MI5 and MI6 on the alert and try to anticipate the most likely targets.'

'Calling in MI5 is one thing,' the Secretary replied, referring to the branch of the Security Service charged with overt counter-espionage. 'But before calling in MI6, would someone please remind me of the reasoning behind what was obviously an exceptionally ambitious and contentious ambush.'

Everyone around the table knew just what he meant. MI6 was the secret intelligence service run by the Foreign and Commonwealth Office. As its links with the FCO were never publicly acknowledged, it was best avoided when it came to operations that might end up with a high public profile – as, for instance, the siege of the Iranian Embassy in London in May 1980 had done.

'The humiliation of the IRA,' said the leader of the Special Military Intelligence Unit (SMIU) responsible for Northern Ireland. 'That was the whole purpose of the Loughgall ambush.'

'We're constantly trying to humiliate the IRA,' the Secretary replied, 'but we don't always go to such lengths. What made Loughgall so special?'

'The assassination of the Lord Chief Justice and his wife the previous month,' the SMIU leader replied, referring to the blowing up of the judge's car by a 500lb bomb in the early hours of 25 April, when he and his wife were returning to their home in Northern Ireland after a holiday in the Republic. 'As Northern Ireland's most senior judge, he had publicly vowed to bring all terrorists to justice, so the terrorists assassinated him, not only as a warning to other like-minded judges, but as a means of profoundly embarrassing the British government, which of course it did.'

'So the ambush at Loughgall was an act of revenge for the murder of the Lord Chief Justice and his wife?'

'It was actually more than that, Mr Secretary,' the SMIU man replied. 'Within hours of the assassination of the Lord Chief Justice – that same evening, in fact – a full-time member of the East Tyrone UDR was murdered by two IRA gunmen while working in the yard of his own farm. That murder was particularly brutal. After shooting him in the back with assault rifles, in full view of his wife, the two gunmen stood

12

over him where he lay on the ground and shot him repeatedly – about nineteen times in all. The East Tyrone IRA then
claimed that they had carried out the killing.'

'And that was somehow connected to the Loughgall
ambush?'

'Yes, Mr Secretary. We learnt from an informer that two
ASU teams from East Tyrone were planning an attack on
the RUC police station at Loughgall and that some of the
men involved had been responsible for all three deaths.'

'Was this informer known to be reliable?'

'Yes, Mr Secretary, she was.'

'And do we have proof that some of the IRA men who
died at Loughgall were involved in the assassinations as she
had stated?'

'Again, the answer is yes. Ballistics tests on the Heckler &
Koch G3 assault rifles and FNCs used by the IRA men at
Loughgall proved that some of them were the same as those
used to kill the UDR man.'

'What about the Lord Chief Justice and his wife?'

'For various reasons, including the reports of informants,
we believe that the ASU teams involved in the attack at
Loughgall were the same ones responsible for the deaths of
the Lord Chief Justice and his wife. However, I'll admit that
as yet we have no conclusive evidence to support that belief.'

'Yet you authorized the SAS ambush at the police station,
killing eight IRA suspects.'

'Not suspects, Mr Secretary. All of them were proven IRA
activists, most with blood on their hands – so we had no
doubts on that score. That being said, I should reiterate that
we certainly knew that the two ASU team leaders – Jim
Lynagh and Patrick Kelly – were responsible for the death of
the UDR man. So the SAS ambush was not only retaliation

for that, but also our way of humiliating the IRA and cancel-
ling out the propaganda victory they had achieved with the
assassination of the Lord Chief Justice and his wife. Which
is why, even knowing that they were planning to attack the
Loughgall RUC station, we decided to let it run and use the attack
as our excuse for neutralizing them with the aid of the SAS and
the RUC. Thus Operation Judy was put into motion.'

'The RUC was involved as well?'

'Of course, Mr Secretary. It was one of *their* police stations,
after all, that was the target. Also, they knew that this was
a plum opportunity to take out some particularly valuable
IRA men, including the two ASU team leaders.'

'So the IRA gunmen were under surveillance long before
the attack took place?'

'Correct, Mr Secretary. We learnt through Intelligence
sources at the TCG . . .'

'The *what*?'

'The Tasking and Co-ordination Group. We learnt through
the TCG's Intelligence that Lynagh and Kelly would be leading
two of the ASU teams against the police station and that
they would be heavily armed. It's true that we were aware
that their intention was not to kill but to destroy the police
station – they knew that it was normally closed and empty
by that time – but given their general value to the IRA, as
well as their direct involvement in the murder of the UDR
man and suspected involvement in the assassination of the
Lord Chief Justice and his wife, we couldn't let that consideration prevent us from grabbing this golden opportunity to
get rid of them once and for all. Therefore, long before the
attack, we had them shadowed by Army surveillance experts
and the Special Branch's E4A. It was members of the latter
who actually witnessed the ASU teams placing the 200lb

bomb in the bucket of that mechanical digger and then driving it to the Loughgall RUC station. We believe that what happened next was completely justified on our part.'

The man known to them all only as the 'Controller' was one of the most senior officers in the SAS, rarely present at Stirling Lines, though often to be seen commuting between the SAS HQ at the Duke of York's Barracks, in Chelsea, and this basement office in Whitehall. Up to this point the Secretary had ignored him, but now, with a slight, sly smile, he brought him into the conversation.

'As I recall,' the Secretary said, 'there were certain contentious aspects to the Loughgall operation.'

'Oh, really?' the Controller replied with a steady, bland, blue-eyed gaze, looking like an ageing matinée idol in his immaculate pinstripe suit and old school tie. 'What are those?'

'For a start, there are a lot of conflicting stories as to what actually happened during that ambush. Why, for instance, would seasoned IRA terrorists open fire, at 7.20 p.m., on an RUC station widely known to keep limited hours and to close completetly at 7 p.m.? Why didn't they just bomb it and run?'

'I know what you're suggesting, Mr Secretary, but you're wrong. Rumours that the SAS opened fire first are false. At least two of the IRA men – we believe Kelly and his driver, Donnelly – stepped down from the cabin of the Toyota and opened fire on the police station with their assault rifles.'

'Even believing it to be closed and empty?'

'Yes. It seems odd, but that's what happened. The only explanation we can come up with is that Kelly and the other ASU team leader, Jim Lynagh, had an argument as to what tactics to use. That argument probably continued in the van as the terrorists travelled from their hide in the farmyard near the border to Loughgall. Kelly became impatient or lost

15

his temper completely and decided to terminate the argument by getting out and opening fire on the police station, using it as the signal for the other men to start the attack. We can think of no other explanation for that rather pointless action. Either that or it was an impulsive act of bravado, though the general belief is that Kelly was too experienced a man to succumb to that.'

'And it's for that very reason that there are those who refuse to believe that the IRA opened fire first. They say that Kelly was simply too experienced to have fired his assault rifle at an empty police station he intended to destroy with a bomb.'

'My men swear that the IRA opened fire first and that's in their official report.'

'But your men *were* there to set up an ambush.'

'Well, Mr Secretary, we'd been briefed by British Intelligence that the mission was to be an OP/React. In other words, an observation post able to react.'

'In other words,' the Secretary said drily, 'an ambush. Isn't that more accurate?'

'Yes, Mr Secretary, it is. An OP/React is a coded term for an ambush.'

'And we can take it from the wide variety of weapons and the extraordinary amount of ammunition used by the SAS – about a thousand bullets fired, I believe, in a couple of minutes – that the purpose of the exercise was to annihilate those men.'

'I believe the proper word is "neutralize",' the SMIU leader put in, feeling obliged to defend the operation he had helped to set up.

'My apologies,' the Secretary responded testily. 'To *neutralize* those men. Does that explain why there were ambush teams outside as well as inside the building and why some of the local townsfolk were shot up – with one actually killed – by the SAS?'

'Those were unfortunate accidents,' the Controller replied firmly, 'but they weren't caused by an unnecessary display of fire-power on our part. The GPMG assault groups positioned in the copse were placed there because it was believed at the time – erroneously, as it turned out – that the IRA bomb team would approach the police station by way of the football pitch across the road from Armagh. The reason for having other troopers hidden elsewhere, including behind the wall of the church and in the town itself, is that we had also been informed that the IRA bomb would be set off by a timer or a remote-control device. We therefore had to be prepared to shoot at any point where a terrorist, irrespective of where he was located, looked as if he was about to do a button-job.'

The Secretary looked perplexed.

'Detonating the bomb by a small, radio-control device hidden on the person and usually activated by a simple button,' the SMIU leader explained. 'Which means it can be done by a demolitions man some distance from the target. In the event, a simple fuse was used, which meant that those placing the bomb at Loughgall had to stay with it until the last moment and then personally light the fuse.'

'That explanation doesn't help us,' the Secretary said, sounding aggrieved. 'The widow of that dead man, now left with three fatherless children, is claiming compensation from our government and will doubtless get it, albeit in an out-of-court settlement.'

'That man wasn't the first, and he won't be the last, civilian casualty in the war in Northern Ireland.' Again, the shadowy SAS Controller was being firm and not about to take the blame for an action he still deemed to have been justified. 'Sometimes these unfortunate accidents can't be avoided.'

'True enough,' the Secretary admitted with a soulful sigh. 'So, let's forget about Loughgall and concentrate on what we believe it will lead to: a bloody act of retaliation by the IRA.'

'Do you know what they're planning?' the Controller asked him.

'We have reason to believe that the target will be soft,' the SMIU man replied on behalf of the Secretary, 'and either in southern Spain or Gibraltar – the first because it has thousands of British tourists as potential victims, the second because the IRA have often publicly stated that it is a potential "soft target" and, even better from their point of view, one strongly identified with British imperialism.'

'Do you have any specific grounds for such suspicions?'

'Yes. We've just been informed by the terrorist experts from the Servicios de Información in Madrid that yesterday two well-known and experienced IRA members, Sean Savage and Daniel McCann, arrived in Spain under false names. Savage is a shadowy figure of no proven IRA affiliations, though he's been under RUC surveillance for a long time and is certainly suspected of being one of the IRA's best men. McCann is widely known as 'Mad Dan' because of his reputation as an absolutely ruthless IRA fanatic up to his elbows in blood. It's our belief that their presence in Spain, particularly as they're there under false passports, indicates some kind of IRA attack, to take place either in Spain – as I said before, because of the enormous tourist population, presently running at about a quarter of a million – or in their oft-proclaimed soft target of Gibraltar. If it's the Rock, where there are approximately fifteen hundred service personnel, then almost certainly it will be a military target.'

'Do we know where they are at the moment?' the Controller asked.

'No,' the SMIU leader replied, sounding slightly embarrassed. 'We only know that they flew from Gatwick to Málaga. Though travelling under false passports, they were recognized by the photos of criminal and political suspects held by the security people at Gatwick. However, when we were informed of their presence at Gatwick, we decided to let them fly on to Spain in order to find out what they were up to. Once in Spain, they were supposed to be tailed by the Spanish police, who unfortunately soon lost them. Right now, we only know that they hired a car at Málaga airport and headed along the N340 towards Torremolinos or somewhere further in that direction. The Spanish police are therefore combing the area between Torremolinos and Algeciras and, of course, we're checking everyone going in and out of Gibraltar. I'm sure we'll find them in good time.'

'So what happens when they're found?' the Controller asked.

'Nothing,' the SMIU man told him. 'At least not just yet. We just want to observe them and ascertain what they're planning. Should they remain in the Costa del Sol, then naturally we must be concerned for the safety of its thousands of British residents and tourists. On the other hand, if they cross the border into Gibraltar, our suspicions about the Rock as their soft target will be, if not actually confirmed, then certainly heightened.'

'What if they simply have a holiday and then fly back to Northern Ireland?' the Controller asked.

'We'll let them go, but keep them under surveillance, whether it be in the Province or somewhere else. We're convinced, however, that they're not on the Costa del Sol to get a suntan. We think they're there to gather information about a particular

19

target – and our guess is that they'll materialize quite soon on Gib.'

'To cause damage?'

'Not now, but later,' the SMIU leader said. 'These men have entered Spain with no more than suitcases, so unless they meet up with someone, or pick up something *en route*, we have to assume that this is purely a scouting trip.'

'Given all the questions you've just asked me about the Loughgall affair,' the Controller said, smiling sardonically at the Secretary, 'can I take it that you're considering future SAS involvement?'

'Yes.' The Secretary leant across his desk to stare intently at the Controller. 'If the terrorist outrage is going to be on Spanish territory, the scenario will place enormous constraints upon us – notably in that we'll be totally dependent on the cooperation of the Spanish police and the Servicios de Información. This problem, unfortunately, will not go away if the IRA plan their outrage for the Rock, since any attack there will almost certainly have to be initiated on the Spanish side of the border, which will again make us dependent on Spanish police and Intelligence. Either way, they won't be happy with any overt British military or Intelligence presence on the scene; nor indeed with the possibility of an essentially British problem being sorted out, perhaps violently and publicly, on Spanish soil. For this reason, as with the Iranian Embassy siege, we'll be caught between making this a police matter – in this case the Spanish or Gibraltar police – or a military matter undertaken by ourselves. If it's the latter, we'll have to persuade the Spanish authorities that we can contain the matter as an anti-terrorist operation run by a small, specially trained group of men, rather than having any kind of full-scale action by the regular Army. That small group of men would have to be the SAS.'

'Quite right, too,' the Controller said.

The Secretary smiled bleakly, not happy to have handed the Controller a garland of flowers. 'While undoubtedly your SAS have proved their worth over the years, they are not the only ones to have done so: the Royal Marines, for instance, could possibly undertake the same, small-scale operation.'

'Not so well,' the Controller insisted. 'Not with a group as small as the one you'll need for this particular task.'

'Perhaps, perhaps not,' the Secretary said doubtfully. 'I have to tell you, however, that I've chosen the SAS not just because of their counter-terrorism talents but because they're experienced in working closely with the police – albeit usually the British police – and, more importantly, because the Iranian Embassy job has given them the highest profile of any of the Special Forces in this or indeed any other country.'

'Not always a good thing,' the Controller admitted, for in truth he detested the notoriety gained by the SAS through that one much-publicized operation.

'But good in this case,' the Secretary told him, 'as the Spanish authorities also know of your Regiment's reputation for counter-terrorist activities and will doubtless respond warmly to it.'

'So at what point do we step in?' the Controller asked, now glancing at the SMIU leader, who was the one who would make that decision.

'This has to remain a matter between British Intelligence and the Servicios de Información until such time as the terrorists actually make their move. Once that appears to be the case, the decision will have to be taken as to whether the Spanish police, the Gibraltar police or the SAS will be given responsibility for dealing with it. In the meantime, we want you to discuss the two possible scenarios – the Spanish mainland or Gibraltar – with your Intelligence people at SAS HQ and devise suitable options for both. When the time comes we'll call you.'

'Excellent,' the Controller said. 'Is that all?'

'Yes,' the Secretary told him.

Nodding, the Controller, the most shadowy man in the whole of the SAS hierarchy, picked up his briefcase, straightened his pinstripe suit, then marched out of the office, to be driven the short distance to the SAS HQ at the Duke of York's Barracks, where he would make his contingency plans.

A man of very strong, sure instincts, he knew already what would happen. The SAS would take over.

2

After removing his blood-smeared white smock and washing the wet blood from his hands in the sink behind the butcher's shop where he worked, Daniel McCann put on his jacket, checked the money in his wallet, then locked up and stepped into the darkening light of the late afternoon. The mean streets of Republican Belfast had not yet surrendered to night, but they looked dark and grim with their pavements wet with rain, the bricked-up windows and doorways in empty houses, and the usual police checkpoints and security fences.

Though only thirty, 'Mad Dan' looked much older, his face prematurely lined and chiselled into hard, unyielding features by his murderous history and ceaseless conflict with the hated British. In the hot, angry summer of 1969, when he was twelve, Catholic homes in his area had been burnt to the ground by Loyalist neighbours before the 'Brits' were called in to stop them, inaugurating a new era of bloody warfare between the Catholics, the Protestants and the British Army. As a consequence, Mad Dan had become a dedicated IRA veteran, going all the way with his blood-chilling enthusiasm for extortion, kneecapping and other forms of torture and, of course, assassination – not only of Brits and Irish

Prods, but also of his own kind when they stood in his way, betrayed the cause, or otherwise displeased him.

Nevertheless, Mad Dan had led a charmed life. In a long career as an assassin, he had chalked up only one serious conviction – for possessing a detonator – which led to two years in the Maze. By the time he got out, having been even more thoroughly educated by his fellow-Irishmen in the prison, he was all set to become a fanatical IRA activitst with no concept of compromise.

But Mad Dan didn't just torture, maim and kill for the IRA cause; he did it because he had a lust for violence and a taste for blood. He was a mad dog.

At the very least, the RUC and British Army had Mad Dan tabbed as an enthusiastic exponent of shoot-to-kill and repeatedly hauled him out of his bed in the middle of the night to attend the detention centre at Castlereagh for an identity parade or interrogation. Yet even when they beat the hell out of him, Mad Dan spat in their faces.

He liked to walk. It was the best way to get round the city and the way least likely to attract the attention of the RUC or British Army. Now, turning into Grosvenor Road, he passed a police station and regular Army checkpoint, surrounded by high, sandbagged walls and manned by heavily armed soldiers, all wearing DPM clothing, helmets with chin straps, and standard-issue boots. Apart from the private manning the 7.62mm L4 light machine-gun, the soldiers were carrying M16 rifles and had stun and smoke grenades on their webbing. The sight of them always made Mad Dan's blood boil.

That part of Belfast looked like London after the Blitz: rows of terraced houses with their doors and windows bricked up and gardens piled high with rubble. The pavements outside the pubs and certain shops were barricaded with large concrete blocks and sandbags. The windows were caged with heavy-duty wire netting as protection against car bombs and petrol bombers.

Farther along, a soldier with an SA80 assault rifle was covering a sapper while the latter carefully checked the contents of a rubbish bin. Mad Dan was one of those who often fired rocket-propelled grenades from Russian-manufactured RPG7 short-range anti-tank weapons, mainly against police stations, army barracks and armoured personnel carriers or Saracen armoured cars. He was also one of those who had, from a safe distance, command-detonated dustbins filled with explosives. It was for these that the sapper was examining all the rubbish bins near the police station and checkpoint. Usually, when explosives were placed in dustbins, it was done during the night, which is why the sappers had to check every morning. Seeing this particular soldier at work gave Mad Dan a great deal of satisfaction.

Farther down the road, well away from the Army checkpoint, he popped in and out of a few shops and betting shops to collect the protection money required to finance his own Provisional IRA unit. He collected the money in cash, which he stuffed carelessly into his pockets. In the last port of call, a bookie's, he took the protection money from the owner, then placed a few bets and joked about coming back to collect his winnings. The owner, though despising him, was frightened of him and forced a painful smile.

After crossing the road, Mad Dan stopped just short of an RUC station which was guarded by officers wearing flak-jackets and carrying the ubiquitous 5.56mm Ruger Mini-14 assault rifle. There he turned left and circled back through the grimy streets until he was heading up the Falls Road and making friendlier calls to his IRA mates in the pubs of

Springfield, Ballymurphy and Turf Lodge, where everyone looked poor and suspicious. Most noticeable were the gangs of teenagers known as 'dickers', who stood menacingly at street corners, keeping their eyes out for newcomers or anything else they felt was threatening, particularly British Army patrols.

Invariably, with the gangs there were young people on crutches or with arms in slings, beaming with pride because they'd been knee-capped as punishment for some infraction, real or imagined, and were therefore treated as 'hard men' by their mates.

Being a kneecapping specialist, Mad Dan knew most of the dickers and kids by name. He was particularly proud of his kneecapping abilities, but, like his fellow Provisional IRA members, used various methods of punishment, according to the nature of the offence.

It was a harsh truth of Republican Belfast that you could tell the gravity of a man's offence by how he'd been punished. If he had a wound either in the fleshy part of the thigh or in the ankle, from a small .22 pistol, which doesn't shatter bone, then he was only guilty of a minor offence. For something more serious he would be shot in the back of the knee with a high-velocity rifle or pistol, which meant the artery was severed and the kneecap blown right off. Mad Dan's favourite, however, was the 'six-pack', the fate of particularly serious offenders. The victim received a bullet in each elbow, knee and ankle, which put him on crutches for a long time.

While the six-pack was reserved for 'touts', or informers, and other traitors, the less damaging, certainly less agonizing punishments were administered to car thieves, burglars, sex offenders, or anyone too openly critical of the IRA, even though they may have actually done nothing.

As one of the leading practitioners of such punishments, Mad Dan struck so much terror into his victims that when they received a visit from one of his minions, telling them that they had to report for punishment, they nearly always went of their own accord to the place selected for the knee-capping. Knowing what was going to happen to them, many tried to anaesthetize themselves beforehand by getting drunk or sedating themselves with Valium, but Mad Dan always waited for the effects to wear off before inflicting the punishment. He liked to hear them screaming.

'Sure, yer squealin' like a stuck pig,' he would say after the punishment had been dispensed. 'Stop shamin' your mother, bejasus, and act like a man!'

After a couple of pints with some IRA friends in a Republican pub in Andersonstown, Mad Dan caught a taxi to the Falls Road, the Provos' heartland and one of the deadliest killing grounds in Northern Ireland. The streets of the 'war zone', as British soldiers called it, were clogged with armoured Land Rovers and forbidding military fortresses looming against the sky. British Army barricades, topped with barbed wire and protected by machine-gun crews atop Saracen armoured cars, were blocking off the entrance to many streets, with the foot soldiers well armed and looking like Martians in their DPM uniforms, boots, webbing, camouflaged helmets and chin-protectors. The black taxis were packed with passengers too frightened to use public transport or walk. Grey-painted RUC mobiles and Saracens were passing constantly. From both kinds of vehicle, police officers were scanning the upper windows and roofs on either side of the road, looking for possible sniper positions. At the barricades, soldiers were checking everyone entering and, in many instances, taking them aside to roughly search them. As Mad Dan noted with his experienced gaze, there were British Army static observation posts with powerful cameras

on the roofs of the higher buildings, recording every movement in these streets. There were also, as he knew, listening
devices in the ceilings of suspected IRA buildings, as well as
bugs on selected phone lines.

Small wonder that caught between the Brits and the IRA,
ever vigilant in their own way, the Catholics in these streets
had little privacy and were inclined to be paranoid.

Turning into a side-street off the Falls Road, Mad Dan
made his way to a dismal block of flats by a patch of waste
ground filled with rubbish, where mangy dogs and scruffy,
dirt-smeared children were playing noisily in the gathering
darkness. In fact, the block of flats looked like a prison, and
all the more so because up on the high roof was a British
Army OP, its powerful telescope scanning the many people
who loitered along the balconies or on the ground below.
One soldier was manning a 7.62mm GPMG; the others were
holding M16 rifles with the barrels resting lightly on the
sandbagged wall.

Grinning as he looked up at the overt OP, Mad Dan placed
the thumb of his right hand on his nose, then flipped his hand
left and right in ironic, insulting salute. Then he entered the
pub. It was smoky, noisy and convivial inside. Seeing Patrick
Tyrone sitting at one of the tables with an almost empty glass
of Guinness in front of him, Mad Dan asked with a gesture
if he wanted another. When Tyrone nodded, Mad Dan ordered
and paid for two pints, then carried them over to Tyrone's
table. Sitting down, he slid one over to Tyrone, had a long
drink from his own, then wiped his lips with the back of his
hand.

'Ach, sure that's good!' he said.

When Tyrone, another hard man, had responded with a
thin, humourless smile, Mad Dan nodded towards the front

door and said: 'I see the Brits have some OPs on the roof. Do they do any damage?'

'Aye. They're equipped with computers linked to vehicle-registration and suspect-information centres, as well as to surveillance cameras. Also, the shites' high visibility reminds us of their presence and so places a quare few constraints on us. At the same time, the OPs allow members of regular Brit units and 14 Intelligence Company to observe suspects and see who their associates are. This in turn allows the shites collecting intelligence at Lisburn and Brit HQ to investigate links between meetings of individuals and our subsequent group activities. So, aye, those bastard OPs can do us lots of damage.'

'Sure, that's a hell of a mouthful, Pat.'

'Sure, it's also the truth.'

'Do those OPs have any back up?' Mad Dan asked.

'Ackaye'. Each of 'em's backed up with another consisting of two to four soldiers and located near enough to offer immediate firearms support. If that weren't enough, those two OPs are backed up by a QRF . . .'

'Sure, what's that if you'd be writin' home?'

'A Quick Reaction Force of soldiers or police, sometimes both, located at the nearest convenient SF base. And that QRF will respond immediately to a radio call for help from the OPs. So, no, they're not alone, Dan. Those Brit bastards up there have a lot of support.'

Mad Dan nodded, indicating he understood, but really he wasn't all that interested. He was there to receive specific instructions for the forthcoming evening. It was what he now lived for.

'So what is it?' he asked.

'A double hit,' Tyrone informed him. 'A bit of weedin' in the garden. Two bastards that have to be put down to put them out of their misery.'

'A decent thought,' Mad Dan said. 'Now who would they be, then?'

Tyrone had another sip of his Guinness, then took a deep breath. 'Detective Sergeants Michael Malone and Ernest Carson.'

'Two bastards, right enough,' Mad Dan said. 'Sure, that's a quare good choice. Tonight, is it?'

'Aye. They'll be in the Liverpool Bar for a meetin' from eight o'clock on. Just walk in there and do as you see fit. We've no brief other than that. Just make sure they stop breathin'.'

'Any security?'

'None. The dumb shites think they're in neutral territory, so they're there for nothin' else but a quare ol' time. Let the bastards die happy.'

'Weapon?'

'I'll give it to you outside. A 9mm Browning, removed from an SAS bastard killed back in '76. Appropriate, right?'

'Ackaye, real appropriate. Let's go get it an' then I'll be off.'

'Sure, I knew you'd say that.'

After finishing their drinks in a leisurely manner, the two men left the bar. Glancing up at the OPs and fully aware that the pub was under surveillance, Tyrone led Mad Dan along the street and up the concrete steps of the grim block of flats. He stopped on the gloomy landing, where the steps turned back in the other direction to lead up to the first balcony. There, out of sight of the spying Brits, he removed the Browning and handed it to Mad Dan, along with a fourteen-round magazine.

'That's the only ammunition you're gettin',' he said, 'because you've only got time for one round before hightailing it out of there. That also means you've no time for mistakes, so make sure you get them fucks.'

'Sure, that's no problem at all, Pat. I'll riddle the bastards and be out of there before they hit the floorboards.'

'Aye, make sure you do that.' Tyrone glanced up and down the stairs, checking that no one was coming. 'So,' he said, 'I'm goin' home for a bite. Off you go. Best of luck. I'll see you back in the bar in forty minutes.'

'I'll be there,' Mad Dan said.

As Tyrone turned away to go up the steps to his mean flat on the first floor, Mad Dan loaded the magazine into the Browning, then tucked the weapon carefully down the back of his trousers, between the belt and his shirt, hidden under the jacket but where he could reach round and pull it out quickly. He walked back down the stairs and out into the street, in full view of the OPs up above. Bold as brass, he walked alongside the waste ground as the street lights came on to illuminate the dark evening. Emerging into the busy Falls Road, he turned right and walked down the crowded pavement until he reached the nearest parked car. When he bent down to talk to the driver, he was recognized instantly.

'Sure, how did it go, Dan?'

'You know Tyrone. Eyes like cold fried eggs and yammerin' on about the Brits, but he gave me the go-ahead and the weapon.' Mad Dan checked his watch. It was five past eight. 'They'll be in the Liverpool Bar and they should be there now. So, come on, let's get goin', lad.'

When Mad Dan had slipped into the seat beside the driver, the latter said: 'Sure, would that be the Liverpool Bar on Donegall Quay?'

'Aye, that's the one. Drop me off there, keep the engine tickin' over, and get ready to hightail it out of there when I come runnin' out. Then don't stop for anything.'

'I'll be out of there like a bat out of hell. Sure, you've no need to worry, Dan.'

'Just make sure of that, boyo.'

As the car moved off, heading along the Falls Road in the direction of Divis Street, Mad Dan felt perfectly relaxed and passed the time by gazing out of the window at the hated RUC constables and British Army soldiers manning the barricaded police stations and checkpoints. He had no need to feel concerned about the car being identified because it had been hijacked at gunpoint on a road just outside the city, and the driver warned not to report the theft until the following day. The stolen car would be abandoned shortly after the attack and, when found unattended, it would be blown up by the SF as a potential car bomb. The unfortunate owner, if outraged, at least could count himself lucky that he still had his life. To lose your car in this manner was par for the course in Northern Ireland.

It took no time at all for the driver to make his way from Divis Street down past the Clock Tower, along Queen's Square and into Donegall Quay, which ran alongside the bleak docks of the harbour, where idle cranes loomed over the water, their hooks, swinging slightly in the wind blowing in from the sea. On one side the harbour walls rose out of the filthy black water, stained a dirty brown by years of salt water and the elements; on the other were ugly warehouses and Victorian buildings. Tucked between some of the latter was the Liverpool Bar, so called because the Belfast-Liverpool ferries left from the nearby Irish Sea Ferry Terminal.

The driver stopped the car in a dark alley near the pub, out of sight of the armed RUC constables and British soldiers guarding the docks at the other side of the main road. He switched his headlights off, slipped into neutral, and kept the engine ticking over quietly.

Mad Dan opened the door, clambered out of the car, hurried along the alley and turned left into Donegall Quay.

There he slowed down and walked in a more leisurely manner to the front door of the Liverpool Bar, not even looking at the soldiers guarding the terminal across the road. Without hesitation, he opened the door and went inside.

Even as the door was swinging closed behind him, he saw the two well-known policemen, Detective Sergeants Michael Malone and Ernest Carson, having off-duty drinks with some fellow-officers at the bar. Wasting no time, Mad Dan reached behind him, withdrew the Browning from under his jacket, spread his legs and aimed with the two-handed grip in one quick, expert movement.

The first shots were fired before anyone knew what was happening.

Mad Dan fired the whole fourteen rounds in rapid succession, aiming first at Malone, peppering him with 9mm bullets, then swinging the pistol towards Carson, as the first victim was throwing his arms up and slamming back against the bar, knocking over glasses and bottles, which smashed on the floor.

Even before Malone had fallen, Carson was being cut down, jerking epileptically as other bullets smashed the mirrors, bottles and glasses behind the bar. The barman gasped and twisted sideways, wounded by a stray bullet, and collapsed as one of the other policemen also went down, hit by the last bullets of Mad Dan's short, savage fusillade.

Chairs and tables turned over as the customers dived for cover, men bawling, women screaming, in that enclosed, dim and smoky space. Hearing the click of an empty chamber, Mad Dan shoved the handgun back in his trousers and turned around to march resolutely, though with no overt display of urgency, through the front door, out on to the dark pavement of Donegall Quay.

33

Swinging shut behind him, the door deadened the sounds of screaming, bawling and hysterical sobbing from inside the bar.

The RUC constables and British soldiers guarding the terminal across the road neither heard nor saw anything unusual as Mad Dan walked at a normal pace back along the pavement and turned into the darkness of the alley a short way along.

By the time the first of the drinkers had burst out through the front door of the bar, bawling across the road for help, Mad Dan, in the hijacked car, had been raced away from the scene, back to the crowded, anonymous streets of Republican Belfast.

'Out ya get,' his driver said, screeching to a halt in a dark and desolate Falls Road side-street.

Mad Dan and the driver clambered out of the car at the same time, then ran together out of the street and back into the lamplit, still busy Falls Road, where they parted without a word.

As the driver entered the nearest pub, where he would mingle with his mates, Mad Dan went back up the Falls Road and turned eventually into the side-street that led to the pub facing the desolate flats that had the British Army OPs on the rooftops. Though picked up by the infrared thermal imagers and personal weapons' night-sights of the men in the OPs, Mad Dan was viewed by the British observers as no more than another Paddy entering the pub for his nightly pint or two. However, once inside he went directly to the same table he had sat at an hour ago, where Tyrone was still seated, staring up with those eyes that did indeed look no more appealing than cold fried eggs.

'So how did it go?' Tyrone asked, showing little concern.

'The garden's been weeded,' Mad Dan told him. 'No problem at all.'

'Then the drink's on me,' Tyrone said. 'Sit down, Dan. Rest your itchy arse.'

Mad Dan relaxed while Tyrone went to the bar, bought two pints of Guinness and returned to the table. He handed one of the glasses to Mad Dan, raised his own in a slightly mocking toast, then drank. Mad Dan did the same, wiping his lips with the back of his hand.

'Neutralized or semi-neutralized?' Tyrone asked.

'As cold as two hooked fish on a marble slab,' Mad Dan replied.

'Gone to meet their maker.'

'Ackaye,' Mad Dan said.

Tyrone put down his glass, licked his thin lips, then leant over the table to stare very directly at Mad Dan with his cold eyes. 'Sure, I want you to meet someone,' he said.

'Who?' Mad Dan asked.

'A kid called Sean Savage.'

3

Sean Savage loved his country. At twenty-three he was an incurable romantic who read voraciously about the history of Northern Ireland and travelled frequently across the Province by bicycle, his rucksack weighed down with books, as well as food and drink. He had done this so often that he was now considered an expert on Irish history.

With his vivid imagination Sean could almost see the island coming into existence at the end of the Ice Age, some 20,000 years ago, when the ice melted and the land rose up to fight the stormy sea. Cycling along the spectacular crags of the North Antrim coast, he would imagine it being shaped gradually over the years as the sea eroded the land on either side of the rocks, before human habitation was known. Northern Ireland's first inhabitants, he knew, were nomadic boatmen who had crossed from south-west Scotland in 7000 BC and left the debris of their passing, mostly pieces of flint axes, in the soil along the rugged coastline.

Sean was particularly intrigued by those early explorers, often wishing he had been born in that distant time, sometimes even imagining that he had been one of them in a former life. One of his favourite spots was the crag surmounted by the remains of Dunlace Castle, where, sitting as near the edge of the cliff as possible, gazing down at the sea far below, he would imagine himself one of those early explorers, venturing in a flimsy coracle into the enormous cave that ran through the rock to the land.

He was a solitary person, enjoying his own company. Shy with girls and still living with his parents in a terraced house in Republican West Belfast, he filled his spare time with evening classes on the Irish language, cycling all over Northern Ireland, and exploring and reading about the formation of the land and how those early explorers from Scotland were followed by various invaders, including the Christians, the Vikings and, finally, the Normans, who had marked their victories by building castles along the coastline. The remains of those castles still covered the land, reminding Sean that Northern Ireland had often been invaded and was still a country ruled by hated foreigners – namely, the British.

Sean wanted to free his country. As he cycled to and fro across this land steeped in myth and legend – with 'giants, ghosts and banshees wailing through the sea mist', as one of the guidebooks had it – as he read his books and explored the ancient ruins or drank in the beauty of the Mountains of Mourne, the lunar landscape of the Giant's Causeway, or the soothing green glens of Antrim, he wanted desperately to return to the past when Ireland belonged to the Irish. Like his early hero, Sorley Boy MacDonnell, who had boldly captured Dunlace Castle from the English in 1584, Sean wanted to break out of his anonymity and achieve heroic victories.

'Sure, you're just a wee dreamer,' his friend Father Donal Murphy told him, 'wantin' what can't be had. You can't get the past back, boyo, and you'd better accept that fact.'

But Sean couldn't accept that fact. Like many of his friends, Father Murphy knew him as a reflective Irish-language enthusiast, rambler, cyclist, Gaelic footballer and cook. Still single, he neither smoked nor drank alcohol, rarely expressed political views, and was never seen at Republican functions. Not for one second, then, did the priest suspect that Sean was a highly active, dangerous member of the IRA.

The nearest Sean had come to recorded involvement in the 'Troubles' was when, in 1982, he had been arrested on the word of an unknown 'supergrass' who had denounced him as an IRA hit man. Resolute in protesting his innocence, Sean was strongly defended by many friends, including Father Murphy, who all viewed the arrest as yet another example of the British tendency to imprison innocent people on flimsy evidence. Released a month later, Sean returned to his peaceful activities and, in so doing, reinforced the conviction of most of his friends that he had been wrongfully accused.

'They're so keen to find themselves some terrorists,' Father Murphy told him, 'they don't bother with facts. Sure, they only had to run a proper check and they'd have found you were innocent.'

'Ackaye,' Sean replied. 'Sure, that's the truth, Father. They probably didn't care who they arrested – they just needed some fish to fry. We're *all* at risk that way.'

In fact, as only a few, highly placed members of the IRA knew, Sean was a dedicated freedom fighter who would go to any lengths to get the Brits out of the Province. To this end he had joined the IRA while still at school and soon became an expert 'engineer', or bomb maker, responsible for the destruction of RUC stations, British Army checkpoints, and, on more than one occasion, lorries filled with soldiers. Thus, though he seemed innocent enough, he had blood on his hands.

But he was not a 'mad dog' like Daniel McCann and took no great pleasure in killing people. Rather, he viewed his IRA bombings and, on the odd occasion, shootings, as the necessary evils of a just war and despised the more enthusiastic or brutal elements in the organization – those who did it for pleasure.

As Mad Dan McCann was one of those whom he most despised, even if only from what he had heard about him, never having met the man, he wasn't thrilled when, in early November 1987, after receiving a handwritten message from his Provisional IRA leader, Pat Tyrone, inviting him to a meeting in Tyrone's house, he turned up to find McCann there as well.

Sean had long since accepted that once in the IRA it was difficult to get beyond its reach. Like the killing of Prods and Brits, he viewed this iron embrace as another necessary evil and was therefore not surprised that the message from Tyrone was delivered to him by another Provisional IRA member, nineteen-year-old Dan Hennessy, who drove up on a Honda motor-bike to where Sean was sitting on the lower slopes of Slieve Donard, gazing down on the tranquil waters of Strangford Lough. Braking on the slope just below Sean, Hennessy propped the bike up on its stand, then swung his right leg over the saddle and walked up to Sean with a sealed envelope.

'From Pat Tyrone,' Hennessy said, not even bothering to look around him at the magnificent view. Hennessy was as thick as two planks and only in the IRA because he thought it would give him certain privileges in Belfast's underprivileged society. In fact, he would be used as cannon-fodder. As such, he would almost certainly end up either in a British prison or in a ditch with a bullet in his thick skull. It was an unfortunate truth that such scum were necessary to get the dirty work done and that most came to a bad end.

'How did you know I was here?' Sean asked as he opened the envelope.

'Tyrone sent me to your house and your mum said you'd come up here for the day. Sure, what the fuck do you do up here?'

'I read,' Sean informed him.

'You mean you beat off to porn.'

'I read books on history,' Sean said calmly, unfolding the note. 'This is a good place to read.'

'You're a bloody queer one, that's for sure.'

Sean read the note. It was short and to the point: 'Sean: Something has come up. We need to talk. I'll be home at four this afternoon. Meet me there. Yours, Pat Tyrone.' Sean folded the note, replaced it neatly in the envelope, then put the envelope in his pocket and nodded at Hennessy.

'Tell Pat I received the message,' he said.

'Ackaye,' Hennessy replied, then sped off down the slope, still oblivious to the magnificent scenery all about him.

To Sean it was clear that Hennessy loved only himself – not Ireland. He was a teenage hoodlum. Vermin. A former dicker elevated to the Provisional IRA ranks and dreaming of better things. An early grave is all he'll get, he thought as he packed up his things and prepared to cycle back down the lower slopes of the mountain. And it's all he'll deserve.

Disgusted by Hennessy, Sean was reminded of him as he cycled back through the grim streets of West Belfast, where he saw the usual depressing spectacle of armed RUC constables, British Army checkpoints, Saracens patrolling the streets and, of course, the dickers, keeping their eye on the every movement of potentially traitorous Catholics, as well as the Brits and Prods. Like Hennessy, most of those ill-educated, unemployed teenagers were hoping to eventually break free from the tedium of being mere lookouts to become active IRA members and kill some Prods and Brits. As their dreams had little to do with a love of Ireland, Sean despised them as much as he did Hennessy and others like him, including Mad Dan McCann.

He was reminded of his contempt for Mad Dan when, entering Tyrone's two-up, two-down terraced house in one of the depressing little streets off the Falls Road – a strongly Republican street barricaded at both ends by the British Army – he found McCann sitting at the table with Tyrone in the cramped, gloomy living-room, both of them drinking from bottles of stout and wreathed in cigarette smoke.

'Have you come?' Tyrone asked, using that odd form of greeting peculiar to the Ulster Irish.

'Aye, sure I have,' Sean replied.

'You look fit. Been out ridin' on that bike of yours again?'

'Aye. Out Armagh way.'

'Sean rides his bicycle all over the place,' Tyrone explained to Mad Dan, who was studying the younger man with his dark, stormy eyes. 'He sits up there on the hills, all wind-blown, and reads history and studies the Irish language. He's our wee intellectual.'

'Aye, sure I've heard that right enough,' Mad Dan said. 'He's got a right brain on his head, so I've been told.'

'You've met Dan?' Tyrone asked Sean.

'No,' Sean replied. 'I've heard a lot about you,' he added, turning to McCann, but finding it difficult to meet his wild gaze.

'All good, was it?' Mad Dan asked with a leer.

'All right, like,' Sean replied carefully.

Mad Dan burst out into cackling laughter. 'Aye, I'll bet,' he said, then stopped laughing abruptly as Sean pulled up a chair at the table in the tiny living-room. The walls of the house, which belonged to Tyrone's mother, were covered with framed paintings of Jesus, the Virgin Mary and numerous saints.

A real little chapel, Sean thought, for Tyrone's ageing mother. Certainly not for Tyrone. Indeed, when he looked at Tyrone, he knew he was looking at a hard man who had little time for religion, let alone sentiment. Like Sean, Tyrone lived for the cause, but his motives were purely political, not religious. For this reason, Sean respected him. He did not respect McCann the same way, though he certainly feared him. He thought he was an animal.

When Sean had settled in his hard-backed chair. Tyrone waved his hand at the bottles of stout on the table in front of him. 'Sure, help yerself, Sean.'

Sean shook his head from side to side. 'Naw,' he said. 'I'm all right for the moment.'

'Oh, I forgot,' Tyrone said with a grin. 'You don't drink at all.'

'Nothin' but mother's milk,' Mad Dan said. 'Sure, wouldn't that be right, boyo?'

'I just don't like drinkin',' Sean replied. 'What's the matter with that?'

'Men who don't drink can't be trusted,' Mad Dan informed him with a twisted, mocking grin. 'Sure, isn't that a fact now?'

'It's men who drink who can't be trusted,' Sean told him. 'The drink loosens their tongues.'

'And more,' Tyrone said, wiping his wet lips with the palm of his hand. 'It also makes 'em too cocky and careless – too inclined to make mistakes. You stay away from it, laddy.'

The remark offended Mad Dan, making him turn red. 'Sure, you wouldn't be accusin' me of carelessness, would you, Tyrone?'

'Not you, Dan,' Tyrone said, though he had his doubts. 'You can hold your own. I mean in general, that's all.'

Sean coughed into his clenched fist.

'He doesn't smoke either,' Tyrone explained.

'Bejasus!' Mad Dan said sarcastically. 'Sure, isn't he a right wee angel? Where's your gilded wings, boyo?'

Sean didn't bother replying; he just offered a tight smile. 'So what's up?' he asked Tyrone.

'Sure I know you like travellin',' Tyrone replied, 'so I'd like to offer you the chance to travel a bit farther than the tourist sites of Northern Ireland.'

'What's that mean?' Sean asked in his quiet, always deadly serious manner.

Tyrone drew on his cigarette, exhaled a cloud of smoke, then leant slightly across the table, closer to Sean.

'It's to do with the massacre of our eight comrades by those SAS bastards in Loughgall last May.'

Sean knew all about that massacre and felt rage just recalling it. This was a real war in the Province, with real death and destruction, so Sean normally tried to remain objective and not let hatred motivate him or, worse, distort his judgement. Nevertheless, the shooting of eight of his comrades by a large SAS ambush team placed inside and around the RUC station at Longhgall, with a civilian driver also killed and his brother badly wounded, had filled him with an anger that could not be contained. While Sean had not personally been informed of that particular IRA raid, it was as clear as the nose on his face that the Provisional IRA teams involved had timed it to take place after the police station was closed, which meant they had not intended bodily harm, but only to blow up the empty building. The response from the SAS had therefore been out of all proportion to the size of the event – a bloody overkill that had merely confirmed for Sean and other IRA members that the SAS was an officially sanctioned assassination squad acting on behalf of the British government.

'A revenge attack,' Sean said, certain of what was coming.

'Correct.' Tyrone blew another cloud of smoke, then stared intently at Sean. 'We've been thinking about it for the past six months or so and now we're ready to do it.'

'We're going up against the SAS?'

'No. We want something bigger – to humiliate the British government and, at the same time, regain the prestige we lost when our eight comrades were butchered. We want something outrageous.'

'But not on British soil.'

Tyrone smiled in recognition of Sean's ability to read between the lines of what he was saying. 'Right. Not on British soil. We want an outrage that takes place elsewhere and, as well as shockin' the British public, embarrasses the government. That's why you're off on a trip.'

'Where?'

'We want a soft target – not a military target – and as thousands of British tourists visit the Costa del Sol every year, that seems a logical choice.'

'You're going to hit civilians?'

'Aye. That's the general idea.'

'I don't like it,' Sean told him. 'To hit innocent civilians on British soil is bad enough, but it can at least be justified in that we're attacking behind enemy lines and the civilians are innocent bystanders caught up in that war. But to go out and deliberately bomb them in another country isn't remotely the same thing. Sure, it's something that's bound to be viewed as a deliberate atrocity and, worse, one that could outrage the Spanish government even more than the British.'

'Which is precisely what we want,' Tyrone informed him. 'We want them bastard Brits to know that they can't come over here and slaughter eight of our men without expectin' rough justice. An eye for an eye, right?'

'But a civilian target on foreign soil . . .'

'Just what we're after,' Tyrone interrupted him. 'We want the British government to know – we want the whole damn world to know – that the IRA is willin' to take this war to any country where British citizens are to be found in large numbers. We want 'em to know that we consider no one to be innocent – not even ordinary Brits sunnin' it up in Spain. That's one reason. The other is that we'll involve the Spanish authorities in this, whether or not they like it. In doin' so we'll further embarrass the Brits and give them cause to think twice before orderin' the slaughter of IRA men out on missions clearly designed to cause no fatalities. This time *we'll* be the ones to cause a lot of fatalities – mostly innocent citizens – while lettin' the world know exactly why we're doing it: as an act of revenge for Loughgall.'

As Sean was digesting this, Tyrone blew another cloud of smoke, sipped some stout, then asked: 'Have you heard about the assassination of Detective Sergeants Malone and Carson in the Liverpool Bar last August?'

'Ackaye. Who hasn't?'

Tyrone nodded in the direction of the stony-faced Mad Dan. 'Dan here did that one.' When Sean glanced sideways, he saw the assassin grinning with mad pride. Chilled, he had to look away, returning his gaze to Tyrone. 'We ordered those two killed,' Tyrone explained, 'because they spent most evenings drinking in that pub and watching who got off the Liverpool ferry: our own men and the Brits. We believe they were docking our men while givin' the Brits protection when they came off the boat. We also ordered their deaths as an

indication to the Brits that we wouldn't take Loughgall lyin'
down. Which is exactly why you're goin' to Spain, Sean.'

'No complaints from me,' Mad Dan said. 'I could do with
some sunshine.'

After glancing with distaste at Mad Dan, Sean turned back
to Tyrone. 'What's our brief? Do we pick our own target?'

'You don't pick anything. You don't even carry weapons.
This first trip is only for preliminary reconnaissance. You're
to act like normal holiday-makers while you reconnoitre the
area – right along the whole coastline, from Málaga to
Algeciras – and come back with some minimum-risk targets.
We'll take our pick after careful consideration, then send you
back, suitably armed, to do the job.'

'What about Gibraltar?' Sean asked.

'What about it?'

'If the security isn't too tight, it could make an even better
target.'

'Sure, I never even thought about that,' Tyrone said. 'Why
even better?'

'Because it adds a political dimension to the otherwise
bare killing of innocent tourists,' Sean told him.

'How's that, then?'

'Gibraltar's always been strongly identified with British
imperialism and it's still protected by British soldiers. If we
can kill a lot of those, as well as some tourists, the raid would
have a certain logic to the rest of the world. In other words,
outrageous though the bombing would still be – including
the deaths of innocent bystanders – the military nature of the
target would make it less reprehensible to those not directly
involved in Anglo-Irish politics.'

Tyrone stubbed out his cigarette, then sat back in his chair,
clasping his hands behind his head and grinning broadly at

Sean. 'Obviously all that reading up on history hasn't gone to waste, Sean.' He turned to Mad Dan. 'What do you think, Dan?'

'I know nothin' 'bout fuckin' history, except that the Brits are over here an' killin' the Irish. You just tell me where to aim the gun an' I'll squeeze the trigger.'

'Good.' Tyrone turned back to Sean and said: 'Right, then. Include Gibraltar in your travels. If you think we can pull something successful there, then come back with the details.'

'How long are we going for?'

'A week. A seven-day return ticket from Gatwick to Málaga, travelling under false passports. Hire a car when you get to Málaga and play it by ear from there, checking into hotels where and when you want, but for never more than one night at any one place. Naturally, since both of you are almost certainly under British surveillance, you'll be given false passports to use from Gatwick onward. To complicate matters a bit more, you'll fly to London from Dublin – not from here.'

'When do we leave?' Mad Dan asked, clearly keen to get going.

'Tomorrow,' Tyrone told him. 'Come back here at seven tonight and I'll give you the false passports, train tickets to Dublin and tickets for your flight. I'll also give you enough English, Spanish and Gibraltar currency to keep you from having to change money when you're there. If you piss it away in Spanish bars, you'll come back to a six-pack.'

Mad Dan grinned in his evil manner. 'Sure, I give those,' he said. 'I don't get 'em. Who'd six-pack me?'

'Me,' Tyrone said.

The two hard men stared at each other for a few uneasy seconds, as if challenging each other, and Sean realized that Tyrone secretly shared his opinion that Mad Dan was a man who could not be trusted, even though, undeniably, he had his uses.

I'll have to keep my eye on him, Sean thought, when we get to Spain. I may have to muzzle the bastard, like the mad dog he is. This may not run too smoothly.

Eventually, turning away from Mad Dan, Tyrone asked: 'Any questions?'

'No,' Sean said. 'I'll go home right now and pack, then come back here at seven this evening to pick up what's required.'

'Me, too,' Mad Dan said. 'Though I'll have another bottle of stout before I leave.'

Wanting to talk to Tyrone about Mad Dan, whom he viewed as a dangerous partner, but realizing that it was Mad Dan who would get the chance to talk about him, Sean simply nodded, left Tyrone's place, and cycled home.

Irish mothers love their sons dearly and Sean's mother was no exception, but she may have loved him even more because he was so quiet and studious. Therefore she believed him implicitly when he told her that he was taking a break in the rural, Irish-speaking area of Galway, in the Republic, where he was going to stay in a caravan. Long accustomed to her son's impromtu cycle trips, Mrs Savage thought nothing of this latest plan, and gladly packed his suitcase that evening when he was, as she thought, out visiting Father Murphy.

When Sean returned that evening – having been to collect his false passport, Dublin train ticket, return Gatwick-Málaga air ticket, and currency from Tyrone – his suitcase was packed and a supper of cheese and tomato sandwiches was laid out on the table. Sean gratefully ate the sandwiches, drank his cup of tea, kissed his mother on the cheek and went upstairs to bed.

The following morning, he left for his supposedly healthy weekend in the Gaeltacht. Travelling separately from Mad Dan, he caught the train to Dublin, flew from there to Gatwick, from where, using his false passport, he caught another flight to Málaga. Having flown in two hours earlier, Mad Dan met Sean at the airport.

With scarcely a word spoken between them, they went off to hire a car.

4

Nineteen seventy-six was a memorable year in Belfast. In January, after fifteen Protestants and Catholics died in sectarian revenge attacks in one week, the SAS were ordered into the 'bandit country' of south Armagh for the first time, following a spearhead battalion of six hundred British troops, and thus bringing the total Ulster garrison strength to about 15,200. In May ten people were left dead and fifty-six hurt after one of the Province's most violent weekends. In July the British Ambassador to Dublin was killed when his car was blown up by a land-mine. In August three children were killed after being hit by a car hijacked by the IRA and careering out of control after the driver had been shot by British soldiers. Those three deaths led to the launch of the Ulster Peace Movement at a rally of 20,000 Protestants and Roman Catholics. In September Britain was accused by a European Commission of 'inhuman treatment and torture' in its use of 'deep interrogation' techniques on Republican supporters. In October, the Ulster Peace Movement founders were attacked by an angry mob and the Belfast Sinn Fein vice-president was shot dead. In December the wife of the British Ambassador murdered by the IRA the previous July joined the heads of the Church of England and the Roman Catholic Church in Britain in a 30,000-strong peace march organized and led by the co-founders of the Ulster Peace Movement.

Nineteen seventy-six was also the year in which Mairead Farrell bombed the Conway Hotel in Belfast. Ten years later, recently released after almost a decade in prison for her crime, she still dreamed about that bombing. Tossing and turning on her bed, her ravishing long, black hair twining around her pale face, she would see it as she had witnessed it at the time, as if in slow motion: the cracks zigzagging down the walls, bricks and powdered cement blowing outwards, a rain of shards of glass from the windows, then the vivid eruption of flame, boiling smoke and noise, a bass rumbling, followed by a deafening blast, as the bomb did its worst. The explosion made Mairead, then ten years younger, tremble with a mixture of pride and terror.

She had run, but she had not got very far. For even as the first of the nightmares came to haunt her, during those few nights after the deed, when she was being congratulated by her comrades and smiling gratefully to hide her dread, for she was so young at the time, the Brits, particularly those bastards in 14 Intelligence Company, were using their touts to learn who had planted the bomb. They found her, right enough, surprised to learn that the perpetrator had been a woman, and came for her with some RUC bitches to take her away.

Ten years in prison. God, yes, she had paid the price. And only last year, in that bleak September, ten years older but none the wiser – in fact more committed than ever – she had said goodbye to her comrades in the prison and accepted their parting gift of a watch inscribed 'Good luck. From your comrades in Maghaberry, September 1986', and walked out to freedom and a new life with Tom.

God, yes, God help me, Tom. My rock and my cross. Oh, please, Tom, be careful . . .

Everything was a wheel. It all went in circles. She had started as a bomber and now Tom Riley, the man she loved, was out there doing the same. Right now. Sweating somewhere. Planting a bomb. Continuing the war against the hated Brits.

Oh, be careful, my love.

In her dream she saw the exploding Conway Hotel, then Tom walking ghostlike from the flames and smoke, his body on fire, his face melting, calling out to her: 'Help me! Please help me!'

Mairead groaned aloud and awoke, clawing at the sweat-soaked sheet, then let her racing heart settle down and controlled her frantic breathing. When she had surfaced, getting her grip back on reality, she slipped out of the bed.

It was two o'clock in the afternoon. Having trouble sleeping at night, even with Tom, she often slept during the day. She had picked up this particular form of insomnia in prison.

She saw herself in the bathroom mirror. She was still beautiful. The shadows under her dark eyes only enhanced her haunted beauty; her striking long hair framed it. She knew that men found her attractive; she just couldn't feel it. Ever since the bombing, after her decade in prison, she had felt old and used up. Without Tom, when his physical presence was not there to protect her, she wanted only oblivion. She had killed, would certainly kill again, and was savaged by this knowledge. Mairead wanted oblivion.

She bathed, dressed and had an afternoon breakfast of cornflakes and milk, followed by a large cup of tea. Without Tom in it, the small, two-up, two-down terraced house seemed gloomy and unwelcoming, reminding her of her prison cell and the small room she'd had in the convent. For she was a former convent girl, God-fearing, pious, who had bombed a hotel and killed people. In prison, with others of her own kind, other politically committed women, she had not been taught the error of her ways; instead she'd picked up more terrorist skills from those with more experience than her. Mairead had once believed in God and her country; now she only believed in her country and wanted the Brits out.

And yet, although she was still in her early thirties, her belief in the fight for freedom was not enough to sustain her when the bouts of depression hit her. At such times, which now came with increasing frequency, she wanted to die.

Without Tom, she might have died.

But right now he wasn't at home. He was somewhere out there, on the streets of Belfast, intending to plant a bomb in a Protestant hotel on behalf of the IRA. Mairead, who couldn't imagine life without him, could only feel anxious.

Glancing at her watch, she saw that it would be another two hours before Tom's bomb went off. Unable to bear being alone any longer, she put on her coat and left the house, walking hurriedly along the street, past the boarded-up windows and bricked-up doorways of houses either partially destroyed in riots or vacated by their frightened Protestant owners, who had once lived here in peace with their Catholic neighbours. Gangs of unsupervised, often uncontrollable children were shouting noisily at one another in the road, which was littered with broken glass and stones from previous attacks on the soldiers. To Mairead they looked like ragged urchins from some impoverished Third World country and the street didn't look much better. This is what we've been reduced to, she thought, by these British bastards.

Reaching the end of the street, she came to the British Army barricade at the Antrim Road, known as 'Murder Mile' because of the many sectarian killings that took place there.

Watched carefully by unsmiling soldiers, who searched only those entering the street, not those leaving it, Mairead gratefully went through the steel cage beside the barrier and turned along the pavement of the main road, feeling like she was getting out of prison.

Belfast was now a city of steel-caged entrances and barbed wire, so when Mairead reached the fortified pub she had to pass through another double barricade of thick steel wire extending from the roof to the pavement. This, too, reminded her of being in prison. Once inside the steel cage, she made her way along a bunker-like hallway to a locked, reinforced door with a closed viewing panel at eye-level and a bell fixed beside it. When Mairead rang the bell, the viewing panel slid open and a pair of eyes stared suspiciously at her. Recognizing her, the man opened the door and let her in.

Though the interior of the pub was depressingly plain and dirty, it was crowded, smoky and packed with people clearly enjoying themselves and the lively 'crack', or conversation, they were sharing. Seeing that her three best girlfriends, Maureen Tyrone, Aine Dogherty and Josie McGee, were already gathered around a table and drinking a fearsome mixture of vodka and beer, Mairead bought four of the same and then carried them, expertly held between both hands, to the table.

'Sure, I wasn't thinkin' of another drink,' Josie said out of a cloud of cigarette smoke, 'but since you've bought it already . . .'

'Us wee girls just out for a quiet afternoon and now we're bein' corrupted,' Maureen said. 'You're a wicked one, Mairead.'

'Drink up and shut up,' Aine told her. 'Sure, never look a gift-horse in the mouth. Now isn't this grand, girls?'

Though her friends were all good-humoured, Mairead knew that all of them had suffered, one way or another, through the Troubles. Aine's husband, a member of the local Provisional IRA, was serving a ten-year sentence in the Maze after being caught with Semtex and an electrical detonator, leaving her with three small children to support on nothing other then what she got from the 'Buroo' – Social Security. Josie, still unmarried, had lost her father when he was 'executed' in a ditch – shot six times in the head – after being hauled out of his car by some vengeful UDA men as he was driving through south Armagh. Worst hit of all was Maureen, whose twenty-one-year-old son, Seamus, had been shot down in the street the previous year as a punishment for deserting from the 'Stickies' – the official IRA – which would probably not have happened if, as she'd begged him, he'd joined the Provos, who did not expect the same level of commitment. Now, though Maureen was as fanatical as Mairead in her determination to drive the Brits out, she hated the IRA and described them as a bunch of butchers. Sooner or later, if she didn't curb her tongue, she was likely to be picked up by the very people she was criticizing, then tied to a lamppost and tarred and feathered, irrespective of her husband's position in the organization. Rough justice was common here and these women, though secretly suffering, had razor-sharp tongues.

'So how's my wee convent girl from Andersonstown?' Maureen asked, exhaling a cloud of smoke.

'Fine,' Mairead replied, sipping her vodka and beer.

'Sure, if I felt half as bad as you look I'd be six feet under. You still have trouble sleepin'?'

'Ackaye. I wake up in the middle of the night and sleep half the day. I need some of them Valium.'

'You were cut to the bone by all them years in prison,' Josie told her. 'Your heart's been scalded by that, sure it has, and it's racin' too quickly.'

'Where's Tom?' Aine asked.

'Out,' Mairead replied.

'We gathered that,' Maureen said. 'What we want to know is where the wee lad is when he should be in your bed.'

'He just went out,' Mairead said. 'Sure, I didn't ask where he was goin'.'

'You didn't ask because you knew,' Maureen insisted. 'Sure, we understand that. We know why you don't feel good.'

This was true. In fact, Maureen probably knew more about what Tom was doing than Mairead did. She was the wife of Patrick Tyrone and knew as much about local goings-on as anyone else in West Belfast. This was virtually confirmed when she reached across the table to pat the back of Mairead's hand, and said: 'You don't have to bother yourself, love. Sure, Tom will be right as rain. He's done jobs like this one a lot of times.'

'It doesn't matter how often you've done it. Sooner or later your number will come up and either the bastards will get you or you'll be in the soft clay. God, Maureen, I worry.'

'Sure, we all worry, girl, but that's part of the life these days. You probably worry a lot more than most because of your ten years behind bars. You paid a high price for your convictions and now your nerves are on edge. Sure, I've seen it so many times – in the men as well as in the women – and it makes my wee heart bleed. But what can you do? You live with it, that's all.'

'I'm not sure I can live with it. I've been approached – yes, by your Pat among others – to start doin' things here an' there, but I can't work up the courage. I still back the cause – God knows, I love my country – but I have this feelin' I won't survive if I involve myself all over again. I see prison a second time around – or a premature grave – and I don't want either, thanks.'

'You're one of the best, Mairead. You know you'd be looked after.'

'Sure, bein' looked after's no help when the slightest wee thing goes wrong. You're there and somethin' goes amiss and then the Brits are all over you. After that, it's either another ten years in jail or a copper-lined coffin. That thought keeps me awake at night.'

'An' makes you sleep durin' the day,' Josie said.

'Aye, that's right.' Mairead raised her glass, waving it to and fro mockingly. 'And makes me drink this as well. Sure, I'm floatin' on clouds these days.'

'You'll survive,' Maureen told her.

'It's Tom I'm worried about. Ever since prison, I haven't seen my parents and I only step out of the house to come in here and forget myself. Tom's all I've got. Sure, he's blood and bone to me. When he's with me, when he's lyin' there beside me, I can forget all the rest of it. Only then. Only with him.'

'Sure, that's nice,' the romantically inclined Aine said.

'Ackaye, it's nice,' Mairead agreed. 'It's just that when he's not actually there, I'm hardly there myself. And when he's been called, when he's out on a job, don't I just fall to pieces?'

'That's natural.'

'No, it's not. It's not natural to think about death every time your man's away doing his bit of business.'

'It's the business he's in,' Josie told her.

'And the convent,' Maureen added. 'Sure, you were brought up in a convent, your head filled with thoughts of life an' death, God an' the devil, this life and the hereafter, so you always think about extremes and the worst that can happen. Ach, Mairead, you're a basket case.'

They all laughed, including Mairead, though she saw her life unravelling behind her in its simplicity and horror: a happy childhood, early years in the convent school, piety instead of true living, seduction through politics, outrage at the Prods and Brits in Northern Ireland, active involvement in the IRA, the bombing of that Protestant hotel in Belfast; then the ten most precious years of her life wasted in prison and, finally, release and being introduced to Tom by some IRA comrades. Tom was gentle with her. He was also an IRA assassin. He had killed many people in the past, some of them highly placed, and was willing to do so again. Nevertheless, he loved her and she had come to love him.

Mairead's love for Tom sprang out of her fear and was deepened by her knowledge of their shared commitment to the cause. They now had that and each other.

'Let's drink up and get four more,' Maureen said. 'Sure, let's all get tight.'

'I'll second that,' Mairead said.

She was just about to reach for her glass when she saw it tremble a little, the drink slopping slightly from side to side. Even as she noticed this, she felt the slight shaking of the floor beneath her, then heard the muffled blast of a distant, obviously large explosion.

Instantly nervous, she looked at her watch, then said: 'That's him. It's Tom. That must be his bomb.'

'That should give the Prods and the Brits somethin' to think about,' Maureen said, reaching over to squeeze Mairead's hand. 'And give us somethin' to celebrate at the same time. Come on, love, drink up and let me buy you another. Let's make a real day of it.'

'Ackaye,' Mairead said, finishing off her drink and handing the glass to Maureen. 'Sure, that's a grand idea.'

While Maureen was at the bar fetching four more drinks, Mairead chatted with Josie and Aine, glancing around the packed room as she did so. Through the haze of cigarette smoke she could see that some of the other customers were staring surreptitiously at her – some with frank admiration because of her long-haired, pale-faced beauty; others with curiosity and, perhaps, a touch of fear because they knew that she had spent ten years in prison for bombing a Prod hotel. The combination of notoriety and beauty would always make her a marked woman in this tight and paranoid community. Mairead should have been used to it by now, but it still made her uncomfortable.

An exuberant Maureen came reeling back out of the crowd, precariously balancing between her hands four more pints of beer topped up with vodka, splashing some on the floor and giggling hysterically. She was just placing the glasses on the table when the man guarding the door opened it and Patrick Tyrone walked in.

As Tyrone made his way urgently through the people standing up and packed tightly together in the middle of the floor, emerging ghostlike from the swirling cigarette smoke, Mairead noticed that he was not staring at his wife, Maureen, but directly at her. She then realized, with a swooping feeling of horror, that he was looking distraught.

Just about to reach out for her drink, Mairead jerked away without thinking and placed a hand on each side of her face, as if seeking protection. When Tyrone bent down slightly to place his hands consolingly on her shoulders, she heard what seemed to be a roaring inside her head. It was in fact the beating of her heart and the rushing of blood to her head. The pain came before Tyrone spoke, before the words destroyed all hope, and when finally he spoke – 'I'm so sorry, Mairead, but Tom . . .' – she burst into tears.

'Something went wrong,' Tyrone explained. 'We don't know exactly what. We only know Tom didn't manage to get away before his bomb went off. When the building went up, Tom was still inside it. I'm sorry, Mairead. He's dead.'

Mairead broke down completely, sobbing and shaking, and had to be helped out of the pub and back to her lonely house. Though her heart was still beating, though she was still alive physically, in a very real sense she died that night.

When eventually she emerged to the light of day, she was ready for anything.

5

The four-man SAS surveillance team had been in their covert OP a long time and were beginning to hate their own stench. They were in a loft that overlooked the fortified pub used constantly by hard-line members of the IRA and their Provisional IRA groups, as well as uninvolved locals, and had been there for five days, keeping watch on the movements of Patrick Tyrone and the female terrorist they knew only as Mairead. Now, in the early evening of the fifth day, they were beginning to wonder just how long they would have to stay there.

'That woman hasn't done a damn thing since getting out of prison last year,' Sergeant Bill Carruthers whispered as he studied the fortified entrance to the bar across the road through his black-painted military binoculars, 'so I don't know what those bastards in Intelligence are expecting.'

'They think that sooner or later she'll go back to her old game of bombing hotels,' Sergeant Roy Ainsworth replied. 'Particularly since she's fallen into bed with Tom Riley. We all know he's been responsible for some of the biggest IRA assassinations of recent years. She's also heavily influenced by Tyrone, and he's good at the soft push. If he pushes her gently enough in the right direction, she'll eventually make a move. When she does, she'll be dangerous.'

'My bet's on that Riley,' Corporal Mark Dymock said. Trained at the Hereford and Royal Signals establishments at Catterick and Blandford, he was fiddling with his Landmaster III hand-held transceiver. 'I've been listening to those two all week and they're a pretty hot item. So if Riley asks her to go back to work, I reckon she'll do what he says.'

'Hear, hear,' Corporal Ralph Billings said.

The four men had moved into the loft of a house occupied by a tout, Mick O'Mara, under cover of a British Army cordon-and-search sweep of the lower Falls Road, with particular emphasis on this particular street because it harboured not only the pub opposite, but also the Tyrones' house, located further along. The dawn sweep had been conducted just like the real thing, with hundreds of troops being brought into the area in Saracen armoured cars, armoured troop carriers and RUC paddy-wagons. After rumbling ominously past police stations and army barricades along the Falls Road in the early-morning darkness, the vehicles had divided into three separate columns that swept into three parallel side-streets to begin the search. Within minutes the area was surrounded and the streets were blocked off.

Pouring out of the various vehicles, some two hundred troops in DPM clothing, body armour and helmets, armed with a variety of weapons, made a great show of searching every house, after throwing their occupants temporarily out into the street and frisking the men on the pavements, in full view of their wives and kids and, in most cases, while being attacked by excited children and dickers throwing stones, bottles and other debris.

During this noisy confusion a team of Parachute Regiment troops had entered one of the houses under the pretence of searching it, but instead they had gone ahead of the SAS men up a stepladder and then 'mouseholed' along the single loft space of the terrace to O'Mara's loft, where they had deposited most of the heavier surveillance equipment. When they had come back down the ladder and were making a great show of violently searching the house – sweeping bric-à-brac off cupboards and shelves, emptying the contents of drawers on to the floor – the four-man SAS team, carrying their personal weapons and kit, were able to clamber up the ladder and crawl along to the same loft. Even as the trapdoor was being tugged shut by one of the paratroopers, the SAS men were setting up their surveillance and survival equipment. By the time the mock cordon-and-search sweep was over, they had settled in.

It had been a grim five days, but they had been rigorously trained for this kind of surveillance. Included in their personal kit were ten days' high-calorie rations, mostly chocolate and sweets because they could not use their hexamine stoves or otherwise cook or heat anything in the loft. In pouches on their belts they carried spare underwear and the usual first-aid kit; also, on the belt itself, a torch and binoculars. They carried as well extra ammunition for the only weapons they were allowed in the OP: their standard-issue 9mm Browning High Power handgun and the short 9mm Sterling MK5 sub-machine-gun with retractable butt and thirty-four round magazine. The rest of their equipment, which had been brought in before their arrival by the paratroopers, consisted of water in plastic bottles; spare radio batteries; medical packs; extra ammunition; 35mm SLR cameras and film; tape-recorders; thermal imagers and night-vision telescopes; an advanced laser audio-surveillance transceiver; ball-points and plastic-backed notebooks; sleeping bags; packs of moisturized cloths for cleaning their faces and hands; towels; toilet paper; and sealable plastic bags for their excrement and urine.

For the past five days they had been spying on the fortified entrance to the pub through a peep-hole created by removing a slate nail in the roof and replacing it with a rubber band that allowed the slate to be raised and lowered to accommodate the naked eye, binoculars, cameras or the thermal imager. Their visual surveillance was complemented by miniature fibre-optic probes that had been placed at four o'clock in the morning in narrow holes drilled in three of the walls of the pub, both sides and rear, to pick up as much of the conversation as possible. This wasn't all that much because, although the laser system was highly advanced, the conversation of individuals was usually drowned by the general babble of the drinkers.

Nevertheless, with the aid of the hand-held thermal imager weighing only 11lb, the fibre-optic probe inserted in the wall of the pub and transmitting aural data back to the laser system in the loft, and the many photos taken with a 35mm Nikon F3HP camera, fitted with a Davies Minimodulux image intensifier, of everyone entering or leaving the pub by night or by day, they were gradually building up a comprehensive picture of the kind of activity and conversation taking place there.

From this, and from other pieces of moderately valuable information, they were able to glean the knowledge that the female IRA bomber went to the pub every afternoon and usually stayed until about six o'clock, which was, for local people, just before dinner-time.

'As regular as clockwork,' Corporal Dymock observed. 'She must like to feed her face.'

'Fried fish and spuds,' Corporal Billings replied. 'It'll be a Good Friday diet every day of the week.'

'She looks good on it,' Dymock said.

'A luscious piece,' Billings agreed.

'You could spot her a mile away with that long hair,' Sergeant Ainsworth added. 'It's really quite striking.'

'She doesn't look like she could hurt a fly,' Billings said. 'I mean, I can't imagine her bombing a bloody hotel or anything else.'

'Well, she did,' Sergeant Carruthers told him, 'and she might do so again. So shut your traps and pay attention to your work. We want to hear what she says in there.'

Though none of the recorded conversations between Mairead and her friends, usually women, revealed anything of much interest, the soldiers learnt from the banter between her and Maureen Tyrone that the former's boyfriend was planning a bombing for the near future. What they had not been able to ascertain was the exact nature and location of the target, as these had never been mentioned during the daily get-togethers between Mairead and her friends.

'You can tell from the conversations that those women know when their men are on a job,' Carruthers said, 'but I don't think they're given any details. Either that or they simply make a point of never discussing precise details with each other – certainly not in the pub. That bastard Riley's planning something, but that's about all we know. Keep listening. Keep watching. Maybe, when the pieces come together, we'll be able to suss what he's planning before he actually pulls it off.'

Apart from that glimmer of information about a possible bombing in the near future, the men in the loft could do little but endure days of dreadful discomfort and a tedium so absolute that it could only be broken by the less than exciting revelations of their visual and audio surveillance.

One day in the tiny loft was enough to make all of them feel grubby, exhausted and claustrophobic. Also, though it was freezing cold, the need to be quiet and not let O'Mara's neighbours suspect their presence had forced them to take off their boots and wear only extra layers of socks – as, indeed, they were doing with their underclothes. Nutritionally, the situation was even worse. As no food could be cooked, they were forced to subsist on dry high-calorie rations, such as biscuits, cheese, chocolate and sweets. Although they had a couple of vacuum flasks of hot tea and coffee, they had to limit themselves to one hot drink a day and, for the rest of the time, tepid water from the plastic water bottles.

As there was nowhere to wash, they could only clean themselves with moisturized cloths and freshen their teeth as best they could with chewing gum. Even worse, as the loft was not divided from the other lofts in the terrace, the corresponding space in the adjoining house had to be used as a toilet. For this purpose the men used plastic bags, which they had to seal and store carefully after use. Since they had to do this in full view of one another, they found this aspect of the OP particularly humiliating.

'We should at least be able to shit in private,' Dymock complained. 'If I'd known I'd have to do it in front of you lot, I'd never have volunteered.'

'As I recall,' Carruthers reminded him, 'you only volunteered by not refusing when I submitted your name for the detail – so don't come it with me, son.'

'You've always been so kind to me, Sarge,' said the corporal. 'Now please let me shit in peace.'

Even during the night they found no respite from the discomforts of the day. Given the lack of space, let alone floorboards – they made their way about the place by hopping from one joist to the other – they could only sleep sitting upright, against the brick walls, with a blanket wrapped around them for warmth and a cushion under the backside. They rested two at a time, one sleeping, the other just relaxing, though the second was compelled to keep a constant eye on the first in case he talked or cried out in his sleep, alerting the neighbours on either side.

'I think we should put a clothes peg on Ralph's nose,' Dymock said of his fellow-corporal, 'to stop him from snoring.'

'I don't snore,' Billings shot back.

'You snore like an elephant bellowing,' Dymock insisted, 'and it could get us all killed. That's why I have to keep waking you to prevent us from being discovered and getting our balls shot off.'

'Obviously that's why I'm so exhausted,' Billings said. 'I never get any sleep.'

Temporary escape from the claustrophobia of the loft came through communication via the hand-held transceiver, operating in the VHF/UHF frequency range, or through the UHG band on their portable radio. The men were able to do this when manning the surveillance equipment because they were equipped with Davies M135b covert microphones with standard safety-pin attachment and ear-worn receivers, positioned on the collar of the jacket, with the on-off switch taped to the wrist. One of these was tuned in to the military command network at Lisburn; the other to the surveillance network, including two Quick Reaction Force units located in two separate RUC stations nearby and prepared to rescue them should their presence in the loft be discovered by the neighbours and the information passed on to the IRA.

'If I'm hearing right,' Carruthers said, removing his receiver to scratch his ear, 'Mad Dan's had a few meetings with Tyrone over in that pub.'

'Who's Mad Dan?' Ainsworth asked him.

'He's the bastard who's widely believed to have shot Detective Sergeants Michael Malone and Ernest Carson in the Liverpool Bar on Donegall Quay. He keeps popping in there to see Tyrone. Unfortunately, like the women, they never discuss anything too specific, though both of them keep making veiled references to some job coming up.'

'Maybe they're talking about the planned bombing by Riley.'

'No. They're talking about using some other man – and they've also mentioned Mairead once or twice. I think they have plans for her.'

'With a woman who looks like that, I don't blame them.'

'No, dickhead. I mean real plans. IRA work.'

'Then let's keep listening and watching,' Ainsworth said, 'and maybe, given time, they'll have a slip of the tongue and give something away.'

'That sounds very wise, Sarge,' Billings said, 'but just how long do you think we can stay up here? We're already very low on water and our food's running out. Not to mention the fact that we're beginning to stink the place out. We can't stay here for ever.'

'A couple more days,' Carruthers said, 'then we'll request that they pull us out.'

'Two more days and I'll be stark, raving mad,' Dymock said.

'So, what's new?' Billings said. 'In fact . . .'

He cut his remark short when he and the others heard the distinct sound of an explosion not too far away. All of them jerked their heads around and looked automatically at the peephole, though they couldn't see anything from where they sat.

As the echo of the explosion died away, Carruthers exclaimed softly: 'That was a bomb!' Then he hurried across to the peep-hole and looked out to see a column of smoke spiralling over the centre of Belfast, its base tinged with the red and yellow glow of flickering flames. 'Looks like someone's bombed a building in the centre of town,' he said. 'In the Protestant area. That makes it a Catholic bomb.'

He scanned the area for some time with his black-painted military binoculars and was just about to put them down again, thinking he wouldn't see much more, when the front door of a house further along the street opened and Tyrone emerged, hurried along the pavement and went into the pub. He was, Carruthers noticed, unusually tense.

'Tyrone's just dashed into the pub,' the sergeant told the rest of the men, 'and he looks pretty upset. Listen carefully, Dymock.'

Unfortunately, Dymock could only hear the general babble of those inside – not specific conversation. He was informing Carruthers of this fact when the pub door opened and Mairead emerged, sobbing profoundly and being supported on either side by the Tyrones. They helped the distraught woman along the street, passing their own house and finally disappearing from view.

'Obviously Tyrone went into that pub to give some news to Mairead,' Carruthers said. 'And whatever it was, it was bad enough to reduce her to tears. I think they're taking her home now. Dymock, get on that Landmaster, contact HQ and find out what's happening.'

Dymock did so, listened intently to what he was being told, then turned the transceiver off and said: 'Wouldn't you know it? That stupid bastard Riley's been found dead in the ruins of the hotel he's just blown up. They think he mistimed it and the bomb went off before he could leave the building. So the dumb fuck blew himself up along with the hotel. That's why Mairead's crying.'

'Jesus Christ!' Carruthers hissed, then stared through the peep-hole at the pub across the road. 'That should certainly change things down there – and not for the better.'

'That's what Captain Edwards thinks,' Dymock informed him, referring to their young CO, presently located at HQ Lisburn. 'In fact, he told me to tell you that we're going to be pulled out of here immediately and have to pack up and prepare to leave. We'll be taken out under cover of another mock cordon-and-search sweep, early tomorrow.'

'That means something really urgent has come up,' Carruthers replied, turning away from the peep-hole and staring at each of the other three men in turn. 'OK, let's get to it.'

Delighted to be leaving the loft, the men started packing up their kit.

The mock cordon-and-search sweep took place the following morning, just before dawn, with the customary convoy of Saracens, armoured personnel carriers and RUC paddy-wagons pouring down the Falls Road with their headlights beaming into the morning darkness. Once they had cordoned off three parallel streets, so concealing the fact that they were really only interested in one of them, British Army, including Parachute Regiment, troops poured out noisily on to the streets. Wearing DPM clothing and helmets, but bulked out even more with ArmourShield General Purpose Vests, including ceramic contoured plates, fragmentation vests, and groin panels, they looked like invaders from outer space. They were armed with sledgehammers, SA-8 assault rifles, and Heckler & Koch MP5 sub-machine-guns, the latter particularly effective for use in confined spaces. The 'snatch' teams, there to take prisoners, looked just as frightening in their full riot gear, including shields and truncheons.

RUC officers trained at the SAS Counter Revolutionary Warfare Wing at Hereford, wearing flak-jackets and carrying 5.56mm Ruger Mini-14 assault rifles, jumped out of the paddy-wagons and surrounded their vehicles as the soldiers and paras raced in opposite directions along the street, hammering on doors with the butts of their weapons and bawling for the inhabits to come out.

At the same time, British Army snipers were clambering on to the roofs from lightweight aluminium assault ladders, to give cover with Lee Enfield .303-inch sniper rifles. Wearing earphones, they were warned of any likely trouble spots either by officers down in the street or by the Royal Marine Gazelle observation helicopter that was hovering right above them, its spinning rotors whipping up a fierce wind that blew the rubbish in the gutters across the street.

As Carruthers glanced down through the peephole he saw the soldiers roughly pushing angry women and dazed children aside to grab their menfolk and haul them out on to the pavement. Other soldiers were forcing their way into the houses to begin what would almost certainly be damaging searches of the properties. When front doors were not opened immediately on request, the soldiers with the sledgehammers smashed them open. As the male residents of the street, many still in their pyjamas, were pushed face first against the front wall of their own houses and made to spread their arms and legs for rough frisking, the women screamed abuse, the children either did the same or burst into tears, and the dickers farther along the street hurled stones, lumps of concrete, bottles and verbal abuse. Meanwhile, a line of soldiers formed a cordon of riot shields across both ends of the street, to prevent any further advance against the troops engaged in the searches.

'Right,' Carruthers said to the other SAS men. 'The street's been cordoned off and the paratroopers are on their way to give us cover. Pick up your gear and get ready to move out. Lift that trapdoor, Billings.'

The corporal was lifting the plywood trapdoor just as the first of the paras burst into the downstairs living-room, being none too gentle with the furnishings. O'Mara made a great show of protesting noisily for the benefit of any neighbours who might be watching from outside or listening through the walls.

Once the paras were inside, Billings lowered himself down through the hole and dropped on to the landing. Dymock then passed the personal kit, weapons and surveillance equipment down to him. By the time everything had been stacked on the landing around Billings, Dymock was dropping down beside him and the paras were rushing up the stairs, hammering on the walls with the butts of their Sterling sub-machine-guns to convince the people next door that their neighbour was just another victim of British brutality.

'Let's move it!' the para sergeant bawled as Carruthers and Ainsworth dropped on to the landing.

'We're all set,' Carruthers said.

Surrounded by the bulky paras, some of whom had divided the boxes of surveillance equipment between them, the SAS troopers picked up their kit and personal weapons, then let themselves be led down the stairs and out through the living-room, where the nervous O'Mara was staring at them wide-eyed, then out into the noisy street.

They barely had time to take in the two cordons of British soldiers blocking off the street before they were raced across the road, still surrounded and shielded by the well-armed paras. As they ran towards the Saracen armoured car that would take them away, armoured personnel carriers screeched to a halt and disgorged riot-control troops. Menacing in their flak-jackets, Perspex-visored helmets and reinforced leg and arm pads, they charged the crowds of men, women, teenagers and children, holding large shields up high and wildly swinging their truncheons as bottles, stones and other debris rained down on and all around them. Reaching the far side of the road, the SAS men were bundled up into the Saracen, their equipment was passed in after them, then the armoured car, with a personnel carrier front and rear, rumbled off along the street. With the Gazelle circling above, the Saracen passed through a pathway formed in the cordon of soldiers, turned into the Falls Road, then headed back for Bessbrook camp, away from the riot caused by the bogus search operation. Soon the noise of the riot was far behind them, to be replaced by the moaning of the wind over the broad, dark fields of Antrim.

Back at Bessbrook, the four men were informed that they were being returned to Hereford, for special retraining in the 'Killing House' in preparation for a forthcoming, as yet unidentified, mission.

6

Sean and Mad Dan both felt mildly uncomfortable at Málaga airport because neither had travelled outside the British Isles before, neither was used to even the relative warmth of early November in southern Spain, and neither spoke a word of Spanish. Also, they were still wearing their heavy, drab Belfast clothing – grey suit, shirt and tie, black shoes – and had felt out of place in the luggage collection area, surrounded by brightly clothed and suntanned British expatriates, most returning to Spain after holidays in Britain.

'Sure, what a bunch of ponces they were,' Mad Dan said to cover his discomfort as Sean drove them in the rented car along the N340. 'All suntanned an' wearin' their lovey-dovey rags even in November.'

'It's still warm here,' Sean replied. 'And a couple of weeks back, when those expats were just flying out to Britain for their hols, it was probably as hot as hell. So their suntans are genuine.'

'Watch that road,' Mad Dan warned him. 'Sure, these Spanish drivers are madmen. An' you're drivin' on the wrong side of the road, so you'd best be doubly careful, boyo.'

'That I will,' Sean promised. He was in fact feeling a little nervous because he had never driven on the right before and was also confused by the forest of international road signs. Startled by the sheer blueness of the sky, catching glimpses of a luminous green-blue sea between the low hills and white Moorish-style villas to his left, he was already realizing just how dreary Belfast was compared with this Mediterranean coastline. The sky, in particular, seemed so high . . . so immense that he felt disorientated. At the same time he was excited to be there, but tried to contain that, not wanting to forget just *why* he was.

'According to that girl in the car-hire office,' he said, 'Torremolinos is only about ten minutes from the airport.'

'Spoke bloody good English for a Spaniard,' Mad Dan said. 'An' had a nice set of water-wings, too.'

Offended and embarrassed by Mad Dan's remark, Sean felt himself blushing and tried to concentrate on the road, which had two lanes each way and too much traffic for comfort. He saw a sign reassuringly indicating 'Torremolinos', and said: 'It's supposed to be a small place, so we'll have one night there and then move on.'

'Sure, boyo. No problem.'

'It doesn't take long to get from Málaga to Gibraltar – a couple of hours at most, I think – so we'll probably spend the rest of our time here driving back and forth, checking and then double-checking to make sure we don't miss anything.'

'Sure, that's fine by me as well. We could have a quare good time here, boyo, even while we're workin', like. I think it's that kind of place.'

'As long as we remember that we're here to work,' Sean said, rather primly.

'Ackaye, boyo, no sweat.'

Within minutes, before he'd had time to gain confidence in driving on the right-hand side of the road, Sean had taken a wrong turning and found himself swept along in the traffic around a bypass that brought him back to the N340 and a series of signs indicating Benalmádena-Costa, Fuengirola, Marbella, Estepona, Algeciras and Cádiz.

'Sure, where the hell are we?' Mad Dan asked, glancing anxiously from the map spread out on his lap to the sea glittering beyond the white houses on his left, and those raised on the parched hills to his right, many with swimming pools, and the mountains soaring up in a blue heat haze beyond the scattered buildings.

'It's all right,' Sean replied, trying to sound more confident than he felt. 'We've just bypassed Torremolinos by mistake, so we'll leave it until the end of the week and check it out on the way back to the airport. The next stop is Fuengi . . .'

Sean couldn't pronounce the word, so Mad Dan checked the map and said: 'Fooengirola. About another fifteen kilometres along this road, so we should be there in no time.' He raised his eyes from the map and glanced with growing enthusiasm at the sunlight beaming down over the road and the cars racing along it with apparent disregard for personal safety. As Mad Dan had little regard for his own safety, this didn't bother him much. 'Sure, isn't this some road?' he asked rhetorically.

'There's an awful lot of accidents on it, so I'm told. They even call it the Road of Death.'

'Sure, given what we're here for,' Mad Dan replied, 'that's a guare good nickname! The Road of Death!'

Finding his partner more distasteful with every passing minute, Sean concentrated even more on the busy road and was glad to see the sign for Fuengirola looming up. Now getting used to driving on the 'wrong' side of the road, he took the marked slip-road and soon found himself sweeping around towards the town, in the shadow of a mountain bleached by the sun, dotted with more white villas and bright-blue swimming pools and surmounted by what he knew from the map was the picturesque village of Mijas.

The confidence Sean had built up driving from the airport soon evaporated when he found himself in the chaotic tangle of traffic in the centre of Fuengirola, but he eventually managed to find a parking space in a relatively quiet side-street. The two men climbed out, removed their shoulder bags from the boot, and made their way into town, through the square and down to the waterfront, where they meandered along the broad seaside promenade until they came to a small hotel set back behind gardens and palm trees. Entering, they were relieved to find that the receptionist, a pretty young Spanish girl, spoke perfect English and was able to give them a single room each. Once in their rooms, they showered, changed into more suitable clothing, then went out to investigate the town. They were both relieved to find that it was packed with English-speaking residents and that most of the Spaniards working in the bars and restaurants spoke it too.

Luckily, though the November weather was relatively mild compared with the British climate, the short Spanish winter was on the way and the temperature was low enough for them to be able to wander about in a fairly relaxed way. As there were quite a few 'Irish' bars in the town, they had no trouble in striking up conversation with fellow-Irishmen and asking questions that seemed perfectly normal coming from new arrivals ostensibly on a package holiday.

From such casual conversations they soon picked up all they needed to know about potential targets for bombing, notably the hotels frequented by the British. Having ascertained the largest of these, which was located right on the

Paseo Marítimo, or promenade, they wandered along to it, ordered drinks in the lounge bar, and used this as a pretext for a careful examination of the grand, seemingly always busy lobby. Sean drank only lemonade, while Mad Dan continued drinking San Miguel beer, as he had been doing all afternoon in the various Irish bars they had visited.

'Sure, the beer is really cheap here,' he said, by way of justifying his drinking. 'An' it's a quare good wee drop.'

'Just don't drink too much,' Sean advised him. 'We're both here to work.'

'Sure, I haven't forgot that, boyo. I'm taking in what I see here and sayin' this is the right spot. Biggest hotel in town, packed with people, even at this time of year, and dead easy to walk into, with no questions asked. Sure, we could get up from our chairs an' go up them stairs an' plant a bomb this minute without bein' stopped. It's all free an' easy here.'

'It's certainly a possibility,' Sean said. 'Particularly as there don't appear to be any other major targets in town.'

'Aye, that's right. There's only pubs, restaurants an' hotels, except maybe the beach. But now that summer's over, I don't recommend that, like. Not enough people.'

'I agree,' Sean said. 'This is the biggest hotel in town – not the best, but about the biggest, the most used – and we could just waltz in like we did just now and leave a bomb under this very table without it bein' noticed. Let's put it down on our list.'

'Ackaye, let's do that. Now what about dinner? I don't want any of that Spanish shite, so let's find a Brit-run place where we can read the menu.'

'Right,' Sean said.

Ignoring the many excellent Spanish restaurants along the Paseo Marítimo and the streets just off it, they had their dinner in an English-run pub most notable for the tattiness of its furnishings and the simplicity of the menu. Ordering the kind of food they were both used to – fish and chips – with another lemonade for Sean and more San Miguels for Mad Dan, they filled their bellies, then wandered idly back along the promenade towards their own little hotel. But before they reached it, Mad Dan, now the worse for wear from his long day's drinking and constantly eyeing up the sensually dressed young Spanish señoritas, insisted on going for another drink or two.

'Sure, these Spanish skirts go to the English bars,' he said, 'and spend most of the night there. We're bound to pick up somethin' an' have somethin' better to do than just sleepin' it off, like.'

'No, thanks,' Sean said. 'I'm tired and I want to go to bed. Besides, it's not our own money we're spendin', so let's be careful.'

'Bollocks, boyo. That's just shite for an' excuse. Sure, yer just a puritanical wee bugger who's frightened of the wimmen. Now, come on, let's go drinkin'.'

'I'm goin' back to take notes on this place an' then have a good sleep.'

'Sure, you do that. I'm off.'

Back at the hotel, Sean conscientiously made notes on the location and interior of the hotel picked as the most likely bombing target in Fuengirola. He also noted the fact that the town itself was family orientated, rather than singles on the loose and couples out for a good time, which would make it a more suitable target for their purposes. As for the hotel, he noted with equal diligence, it was used mostly by English-speaking residents, and, having practically no security arrangements, was easy to enter. Planting a bomb, either in the large, busy lobby bar or in a toilet upstairs, would present few problems. Few other targets in town would be so easy, but then, in propaganda terms, few would be so valuable.

Having completed his notes on Fuengirola in general and the one hotel in particular, Sean undressed and, just before going to bed, went to the window to stare across the promenade to the sea. After the claustrophobic streets of Belfast, it looked incredibly spacious, even exotic, to him. Wondering where Mad Dan was and what he was up to, and worried about his drinking and general propensity for trouble, Sean went to bed and fell into a troubled sleep.

The following morning, over breakfast in the small dining-room of their modest hotel, Sean was compelled to listen to Mad Dan's boastful talk about how he had picked up a 'bit of Spanish skirt' in one of the English pubs, gone on a lengthy pub crawl with her, and ended up in her bed. Judging by Mad Dan's appearance, it was clear to Sean that he had done nothing other than drink until the early hours, but deciding that discretion was the better part of valour, he did not voice his thoughts.

They booked out of the hotel shortly afterwards and took to the Road of Death again, heading for Marbella. The sun was already high over the Mediterranean, laying its light on the water, and Sean, a romantic in all things, even killing with reluctance, felt that he had almost found heaven and was saddened at the evil necessity of causing destruction in it.

'Beautiful,' he whispered as he drove.

'Sure, you're right there, boyo,' Mad Dan replied. 'You should've tried a bit. These Spanish tarts are as hot as green peppers. Sure I had me a grand time.'

'I was talkin' about the scenery,' Sean told him.

Mad Dan snorted with contempt, though he glanced left and right, first at the glittering Mediterranean spread out to their left, below the highway, then at the soaring slopes of the Sierra de Mijas and the clusters of white dwellings scattered about them. Though the light was dim by Mediterranean standards, it was still strong enough to affect Mad Dan's eyes, more used to the grey light of Northern Ireland and now reddened by drink.

'Sure, I always thought sunglasses were pretentious,' he said, 'but now I see the need for them. This is a quare strong light, boyo.'

'You shouldn't drink so much,' Sean said.

'Hark the herald angels sing. Sure, if that's as good as yer feelin' right now, you're not goin' to feel better later. That's what not drinkin' does for you.'

'We're here on a job,' Sean insisted.

'Aye, boyo, I know that. Just because I went out an' had me a good time, doesn't mean I've forgotten what we're here for. Sure, you should be in the Salvation Army – or in a Prod church – you're so damned puritanical, like.'

'All right, let's forget it.'

Quietly furious that he had to work with a man like Mad Dan, but accepting that his colleague had a well-earned reputation as a shoot-to-kill man, Sean drove on along the highway that skirted the sunlit coastline until they arrived at Marbella, which looked particularly sophisticated to his unworldly gaze. Finding a parking space was particularly difficult, forcing them to crawl uphill through the old part of town, through narrow streets filled with white houses, black-shawled women, noisy children, various delivery vans and other cars, then back to the bustling centre of town again, and finally out of town on the same highway, heading towards Nueva Andalucía. Frustrated, Sean used a slip-road to turn around and drive into town, this time managing to find a cramped parking place where he and Mad Dan were able to pay a gypsy parking attendant and then find a hotel that had its own car park.

After booking in, which was conducted in a mixture of broken English and their own minuscule Spanish, both feeling hot and frustrated, they returned to the parked car. They had trouble getting it out of its parking space and then got lost trying to drive back to the hotel, but eventually managed to do so.

They had breakfasted in Fuengirola at eight that morning, but it was now almost one in the afternoon, and Mad Dan said: 'Lunchtime, bejasus. An' I'm dyin' of thirst, like.'

With a sinking heart, Sean agreed to join Mad Dan for a drink in the hotel's bar. Mad Dan finished his San Miguel even before Sean had finished his Coke; but when he discovered that the beer cost almost twice as much as it had in the beach bars and pubs of Fuengirola, he insisted on having lunch elsewhere. Intimidated by the quiet elegance of the hotel, Sean was only too willing to agree, but had the sense to check his guidebook for the most popular area of Marbella.

'The Plaza de los Naranjos,' he said, hoping he was pro-nouncing it correctly, though realizing that Mad Dan wouldn't know if he wasn't.'

'What's that?'

'The Plaza of the Orange Trees. It's right in the centre of town, just round the corner from here. Sure, that's where most people go, so we'll check it out first.'

'Ackaye, let's do that.'

Sean felt overwhelmed by the sophistication of Marbella almost as soon as he stepped out of his hotel. Making his way to the Plaza de los Naranjos, he was struck by the elegance of the narrow, twisting streets leading off in all directions and by the many traditional shops and restaurants they passed, most of which he would have been nervous of entering, particularly with Mad Dan by his side. In the event, arriving at the square itself, he saw that it was encircled by flower-covered balconies, that the pretty white buildings had elegantly tiled, green-shrubbed patios of the most picturesque kind, and that elegantly dressed people were drinking and eating at tables out in the open, under trees laden with oranges.

'Sure, this is the place, all right, boyo,' Mad Dan said with relish. 'You set something off here and you'd blow the whole place away. Let's sit down and check it out.'

Mortified at the very idea of sitting at a table in close proximity to those suntanned, sophisticated men and women, Sean was just about to protest when Mad Dan, seeing a nearby vacant table, hurried up to it and planted himself in a chair. Seeing that it was too late to do otherwise, Sean did the same, taking the chair facing his despised companion.

'This is the life, boyo,' Mad Dan said, glancing sideways at a young lady wearing a skin-tight T-shirt, a skirt so small it looked like a pair of hot plants, and stiletto-heeled shoes. 'Now isn't that a sight for sore eyes? Sure, a man could die happy here.'

When the waiter came, Mad Dan, after an initial communication problem exacerbated by his marked accent, ordered a beer for himself and a Coke for Sean. When the drinks came, they both slaked their thirst, Sean drinking about a quarter of his Coke and Mad Dan polishing off his beer in one long, thirsty gulp. Wiping his lips with the back of his hand, he called the waiter over and ordered another.

'A good start to the day,' he said, then glanced around the picturesque, sunlit square and added: 'Ackaye. A few pounds of Semtex and sure you'd raze this effin' place to the ground and wipe away all these Brits – them and their suntans.'

'They're not all Brits,' Sean pointed out.

'They're not working-class Irish, that's for sure, so this place would do fine.'

'Where do we leave the device?' Sean asked.

'What?' Mad Dan was obviously distracted by the suntanned legs at the next table.

'It's too open here for the leavin' of anything under a table, so where do we leave the device?'

Temporarily removing his eyes from the young woman in hot pants, Mad Dan nodded towards the restaurant that owned the outside table. 'In there. Sure these dumb effin' Spaniards wouldn't suspect a thing. You just place the device in a briefcase, take a table out here an' order a real big meal, then ask the waiter if he'd mind keepin' yer briefcase behind the bar until you've finished yer meal. Set the timer to ignite the explosive about twenty minutes later, when yer supposed to be halfway through your magnificent repast, like. Then, instead of finishin' the meal, you wait till the waiter's inside the restaurant collectin' more food, and you leave the table an' hurry away before anyone notices. When the waiter returns and sees you gone, knowin' your briefcase is behind the bar, he'll assume that you haven't gone far an' will soon be returnin'. Before the dumb bastard realizes it isn't so – like, say, five minutes from when you've pissed off – the bomb will explode. By which time you're back in yer car and harin' out of this place. Sure, it'd work a treat, wouldn't it?'

Sean sighed. 'Maybe . . . maybe not. I still think it's too problematical an' should be avoided.'

Mad Dan winked at the young woman with the long legs and received a frosty stare in return. Unperturbed, he accepted the fresh beer brought by the waiter, waited until he had departed, then took a sip and picked up the guidebook, where he had left it, opened face down, on the table. 'Sure, what about this here Marbella Club? That's filled with rich and perfumed gits who could do with a scorchin'.'

'That's the whole problem,' Sean told him, fighting hard to stay patient. 'They *are* mostly rich and perfumed – the international jet set. The club's owned by a European nobleman and not particularly British. What good would it do to blow up a club used by a bunch of rich internationals? Sure, it'd do us nothing but harm. Besides, they probably wouldn't even let us through the door.'

Mad Dan snorted at that. 'Aye, yer right there. They'd sneer at us down their long noses an' then call for the Spanish police. Right, boyo, I'll give you that. We need somethin' else.'

'Not this place,' Sean said. 'Not Marbella at all. It's too much an international jet-set place. Sure it has as many foreigners as Brits, which isn't what we're after. Given a choice between here and Fuengirola, I'd take the last any day. At least it's full of retired Brits – and they're the ones that we want.'

'Too right,' Mad Dan said.

'So let's strike Marbella off our list.'

'Aye, I agree. So what now?'

Sean looked at his watch. 'Lunch?'

'Ackaye. Sure, I thought you'd never ask. One of them late, long Spanish lunches, then a bit of a kip.'

'We'll have lunch, then a bit of a siesta, then go out and explore again. We might find something suitable.'

'Sure, I thought you said you didn't approve of this place at all.'

'I don't. But we're already booked into our hotel, so we might as well see as much as possible. Sure, you just never know.'

'Aye, right. What about eatin' here?'

'I don't like it,' Sean confessed. 'It's too fancy for me, like. Let's wander down to one of them beach bars where we can relax a lot more.'

'Aye, let's do that. That waiter's lookin' down his long nose at us and I might break it for 'im. So come on, let's pay up an' go.'

They headed for the beach and then wandered up and down it, bickering about where they should eat. In Marbella, even the beach bars looked a bit upmarket, but eventually they managed to settle on one, mainly on the grounds that it had a multilingual menu from which they could easily order. Sean washed his sardines, chips and salad down with Fanta orange, but Mad Dan, enthralled by the relatively low prices, began with a couple of whiskies, then had another four beers with his meal. Throughout, he talked, ever more drunkenly, about the hated Brits, the even worse Brits over here living off low taxes, the various possibilities they had seen so far for a truly outrageous bombing target, and the differences between him and Sean, whom he accepted as a loyal IRA comrade, but otherwise thought of as a Catholic plagued by Prod-style puritanism.

'Sure, a man who doesn't like his drink or sex has to be missin' somethin',' he explained to Sean. 'Ach, boyo, fer Christ's sake start livin'!'

But Sean didn't want to live. At least not that way. What he wanted was to complete this great mission and find something worth bombing. He tried explaining this to Mad Dan, placing their task in its proper context – a necessary evil, a wrong to make something right, random but faultlessly planned destruction to redress an historical injustice – but Mad Dan wasn't listening. He was lost in the glittering sea, the last few suntanned women on the cooling beach, the beer and the thought of another evening in more expat bars, even here in Marbella.

'Now why would I give a bugger if they're all stuck-up ponces around here?' he asked Sean. 'Sure, they're no better than me when they sit on the pot – and that bein' the common line, boyo, I'll go and sit in their bars.'

'Yer goin' out tonight again?' Sean asked him, unable to hide his anxiety.

'Sure, I am that. You've already said we can't make plans for this toffee-nosed place, these bein' international jet-setters, so what's the point in wastin' the evening in pretendin' otherwise? We'll move on farther along the coast tomorrow, but in the meantime, let's make the most of the trip and make a night of it. Come with me, boyo.'

'No, thanks,' Sean said firmly.

That evening Sean retired again to his hotel room to write up his notes while Mad Dan went out for a night on the Spanish tiles. He recorded in his notes more or less what he had told Mad Dan – that while Fuengirola held possibilities, being dominated by Brits, Marbella was too international to be anything other than counterproductive. He then went to bed, read his guidebook on Spain, memorized a few more words and phrases of Spanish, then fell into a sleep in which the long legs that had so hypnotized Mad Dan mesmerized him too. He did not have a good sleep.

Mad Dan looked even worse the next morning, clearly having drunk away most of his normal sleeping hours, but insisted on boasting, over breakfast, of the great time he'd had with another ripe piece of local skirt. Desperate to avoid such conversations, which always unsettled him, and also very conscious that he had been sent here for a purpose, Sean finished his breakfast more quickly than was necessary and insisted that they get out on the road again before the traffic built up. Groaning, Mad Dan agreed.

Once back on the road in their rented car, Mad Dan, feeling the worse for drink and with his nerves on edge, twitched at every passing police car and eventually said to Sean: 'Do you think those bastards back at Málaga airport fell for our false passports?'

'Sure, how could we be drivin' all this time if they knew who we really were. If they'd sussed when we showed them the passports, they'd have sent us right back, like.'

'Ackaye, I'm sure you're right. I just wondered, you know, if maybe they had us on that list they sometimes check at passport control and, you know, had our pictures there.'

'No, I don't think so.'

'Aye, I suppose you're right, boyo. So where are we goin' now?'

'We'll be stayin' tonight in San Pedro, but first I want to check out Puerto Banus, which I was told contains a lot of boats, many of them British.'

'Sure, boats are bloody easy,' Mad Dan said, 'so we'd be right as rain there. Christ, my throat's like a rasp.'

Built along an Andalusian-style harbour village, Puerto Banus had berths for nearly a thousand boats and certainly had several hundred at anchor, ranging all the way from small motor launches to the magnificent craft of the extremely rich. The L-shaped walkway that ran around the port was lined with many boutiques and outdoor restaurants and bars, from where the customers, while sipping their chilled white wine or *vino tinto* could look on, as if at a cabaret, while bronzed deck-hands, mostly young men and women, tended to the boats or served the tables of the wealthy owners.

'Sure, isn't that a sight to make you want to bomb the place,' Mad Dan said in disgust as he sipped his ruinously expensive San Miguel at one of the outdoor tables. 'A bunch of filthy rich parasites!'

'We're not here to take revenge on the rich,' Sean quietly reminded him. 'Not unless they're British.'

'Sure there's plenty of rich Brit scum out there,' Mad Dan said with some venom. 'Let the others drown with them.'

'This place certainly has possibilities,' Sean acknowledged, though with some reluctance, 'so I'll put it down on our list. Now let's drive on to San Pedro.'

'What about lunch?' said the ever-thirsty Mad Dan.

'It's only five minutes by car to San Pedro,' Sean informed him impatiently, 'so it'll be too early for lunch when we get there.'

'I'm just thirsty,' Mad Dan explained without conviction.

Sean felt that he was quietly taking over Mad Dan, getting used to him, controlling him, and he exercised that control by ensuring that he could not have another lengthy, drunken lunch and instead took him back on the road for the drive to San Pedro Alcántara. There wasn't much to see there – the place was just too small, too unknown to make a big splash – so after a light lunch during which Sean let Mad Dan have one beer – they drove on for another fifteen kilometres to Estepona, arriving there still too early for lunch. Once off the promenade, they found a more authentically Spanish town than Marbella, with *típico* bars, goatherds driving their herds through the narrow streets, and black-shawled older women sitting on hard-backed wooden chairs outside their front doors, chatting animatedly.

To the historically minded Sean it was incredibly romantic, the real, uncorrupted world; but it was not a suitable target for a bombing, since there weren't enough Brits – at least not enough to warrant a bombing outrage. This was still a Spanish town.

The next two days were spent driving repeatedly up and down the coast between Estepona and Algeciras, just across the bay from Morocco, with stops at Sotogrande, San Roque and Carteya, a small village whose sole point of interest – at least to Sean, if not to Mad Dan – was some Roman remains. San Roque was not much better, still being almost wholly Spanish; but Sotogrande had strong possibilities, being a luxury development with two world-famous golf courses and a polo ground.

'Plant a device in *that* place,' Mad Dan said, 'and you'd get attention all right. Sure, it'd make the press worldwide.'

'You could be right,' Sean replied.

That evening, they booked into a ramshackle hotel in the hot, dusty port of Algeciras, from where they had a magnificent view across the bay to the Rock of Gibraltar. Sean was thrilled to see it. From his reading of history – and he did not read only Irish history – he knew that the Rock was three-quarters of a mile wide, two and three-quarter miles long, and 1396 feet high at its peak. He also knew that it had taken its name from Gibel-Tarik, or the 'Rock of Tarik', so named after Tarik-ibn Zeyad, the Moorish general who had captured it in 711 when he launched his attack on Spain. Even more romantically, it had been known by the ancients as one of the Pillars of Hercules.

Sean was enthralled by it.

93

'God, I'm dry as a boot strap,' Mad Dan said, turning away from the window of the hotel lobby. 'Does this dump have a bar?'

Early the next morning, having ensured that Mad Dan, who'd had another night out on the town could not linger over breakfast, Sean drove them both to the romantically named La Línea de la Concepción, a decidedly unromantic town located right on the border of Spain and Gibraltar, and went from there across to the mighty Rock itself. There, they found a little England in the Mediterranean, with bilingual citizens, Spanish-speaking English 'bobbies' wearing traditional helmets, though in shirt-sleeves, shops filled with English products, pubs with English beer, two English cinemas, and even the Trafalgar Cemetery, containing the graves of some of those killed in the Battle of Trafalgar in 1805.

'This is it,' Sean said excitedly. 'This is what we've been looking for.'

'Damn right,' Mad Dan growled.

7

The 'Killing House' is the SAS's nickname for the Close Quarter Battle (CQB) building at Stirling Lines, Hereford. Initially designed and constructed for the perfecting of body-guard skills, it had gradually come to be used for training in counter-terrorist tactics and hostage rescue.

The four men pulled out of Belfast – Sergeants Bill Carruthers and Roy Ainsworth, and Corporals Mark Dymock and Ralph Billings – were all familiar with the Killing House because, as recruits in the final stages of their rigorous Selection and Training, they had each been compelled to attend a six-week CQB shooting course there, expending some five thousand rounds per week on various exercises with personal weapons. These included rapid magazine changes, malfunction clearance drills, shooting on the move and from unconventional positions, rapid target acquisition, exact shot placement, and head shots. Nevertheless, after a few days leave in which they visited their families, the men were sent back to the Killing House to further refine their already sharply honed skills in the use of personal weapons, notably the 9mm Browning High Power handgun.

Until 1986 the Killing House had contained a single room set up to represent the kind of place where a hostage or hostages might be held. Inside the room were live 'hostages' (SAS men) and 'terrorists' (cardboard cut-outs). To make life more difficult for the SAS rescuers, the room was often in total darkness and the rescue team had to burst in and, in less than four seconds, identify the 'hostages' and then shoot only the 'terrorists', using live ammunition. When, in 1986, this dangerous system led to the death of an SAS sergeant, killed by a head shot when he moved at the wrong moment, the whole system had to be revised.

By November 1987, when the four-man SAS team led by Sergeant Carruthers arrived for their further training, the Killing House had two rooms: one containing the 'terrorists' and 'hostages', the other being the one to be attacked by the assault team. The two separate rooms were connected with a sophisticated camera system that gave a 'real time' coverage of events taking place in one room to a life-size 'wraparound' screen in the other, and vice versa. This enabled the assault team to fire at the images of terrorists projected on the walls, rather than at fellow SAS men acting as such. Special low-charge rounds were used and the walls were made of a bullet-absorbent material that prevented ricochets. The whole exercise would be videoed for debriefings afterwards.

However, when Carruthers's team arrived at the Killing House they were not given further training in hostage-rescue tactics, but in the Standard Operating Procedure known as the 'double tap'. This was a method of 'neutralizing' a terrorist at close quarters by firing in quick succession with a Browning handgun. This SOP had been devised by Major Roy Farran during World War Two. Farran taught his men what was then a rather unorthodox triangular firing posture known as the Grant-Taylor Method: legs spread and slightly bent, pistol raised in the two-handed grip.

The SOP was fully developed and used extensively during the highly dangerous 'Keeni Meeni' operations in Aden in 1964. 'Keeni Meeni' is a Swahili phrase that describes the movement of a snake in the long grass: sinuous and unseen. The same term later became a synonym in Africa – and with the slave trade in the Arabian Gulf – for undercover work. The British Army picked it up in Kenya during the Mau Mau campaign of the early 1950s, and from Kenya it travelled to the SAS in Aden. There it soon came to relate purely to the use of plain-clothes undercover work carried out in the crowded souks and bazaars of the town, when the SAS men, wearing Arab *futahs* and with faces dyed brown, either drove around in unmarked 'Q' cars to pick up terrorists alive and bring them back for questioning or engaged them in CQB and shot them using the 'double tap'.

Though the 'double tap' originally meant two shots fired in quick succession, Major Farran insisted that his men be able to put six rounds through a playing-card at fifteen yards. Eventually, when it was realized that terrorists often carried sophisticated remote detonation devices and that two shots were often insufficient to stop them before they ignited their bomb, the 'double tap', while retaining its original title, evolved into a method of delivering sustained and accurate fire – up to fourteen rounds from a Browning in under three seconds. The troops were taught always to aim at the body and to use the sustained fire-power as a way of keeping the terrorist's hands away from any weapons or remote-control button that he or she may have been carrying.

When Carruthers and his team arrived back in Hereford they were given no information about the nature of the mission they were being prepared for, other than that it would involve

CQB and could be highly dangerous. Told that they would be retraining in the Killing House, they had expected to have to don Bristol body armour with high-velocity ceramic plates, S6 respirator masks, black ballistic helmets and skin-tight aviator's gloves in order to undergo Counter Revolutionary Warfare (CRW) training. Instead, they were instructed by their young CO, Captain Mike Edwards, who had returned from Belfast to Hereford with them, to wear only jeans, a shirt and a light jacket, and to holster their Browning in the cross-draw position under the jacket.

Thus dressed, they were sent into the Killing House for days on end, to perfect their already highly developed skills at the double tap, using the 'nine-milly', as the Browning was widely known. Though they were not training for hostage-rescue work, they still had to work with 'hostages' and 'terrorists' in the form of either dummy figures bearing painted weapons and popping out from behind open doors and window frames, or images projected on the walls of the second room. The idea was to quicken the reactions of the SAS men in differentiating between a terrorist and a hostage, avoiding the shooting of the latter by mistake.

Carrying out this exercise repeatedly, hour after hour, was bad enough, but it was made even worse by the fact that once the dummy figures had been stitched with low-velocity bullets, the men then had to paste paper patches over the holes in the figures, so that the targets could be used again for exactly the same routine. This, even more than the repetitive exercise, nearly drove them all crazy.

'I feel like an interior decorator,' Dymock complained. 'Or a kid in a nursery school. What a waste of time!'

'Stop whining and get on with the job,' Ainsworth told him. 'We haven't got all day.'

'Yes, we have,' Billings retorted. 'We've been doing this all day every day of the week for two weeks now. I'm going spare, Sarge.'

'*I'll* go spare if you don't shut your mouth,' Carruthers told him, 'and give us some peace. None of us like doing this, but it has to be done, so be quiet and get on with it.'

'Yes, boss!' both corporals piped.

For the first few weeks, Carruthers and the others completed the exercises by shouting instructions or warnings at one another as the dummy figures popped out from behind walls, opening doors or up into view in window frames. However, once their skills in this had been honed to a fine pitch, they were given Davies M135b miniature microphones, attached to a covert ear-worn receiver and two miniature radios, operated by an on-off switch taped to the wrist. With this virtually invisible means of communication, the men were able to communicate not only with each other, but with the Drill Instructors checking their activities from outside the Killing House. In the event of a real operation, however, one of each pair of radios would be tuned into the military command network, the other to the surveillance network.

'You sound like a Dalek through this earpiece,' Dymock told Billings when they were taking a break back in the sleeping quarters of the eight-legged dormitory area known as the 'spider'. 'You sound all distorted.'

'I *am* distorted,' Billings replied. 'My whole body is distorted by all that turning and twisting to get off the double taps. I feel bruised and aching all over. I think I'm misshapen.'

'If you didn't drink so much in Hereford,' Ainsworth informed him, 'you wouldn't be feeling so bruised and battered, and you wouldn't be out of shape. Now me, if I was in charge of you, I'd work you to death.'

'I think I'm dead already, Sarge.'

'You're just a limp-wristed ponce.'

'My mother would take offence at that description, Sarge, and I greatly respect her views.'

'A mother's boy,' Sergeant Ainsworth said.

'A fairy,' Sergeant Carruthers added.

'I'm a man among men,' Billings replied. 'I just don't boast about it.'

'That's because you've got nothing to boast about,' Dymock chipped in, although he instinctively sided with his mate against the NCOs in their customary exchange of bullshit.

Once equipped with the covert communications equipment, the four men were sent into a Killing House plunged into darkness, where they had no time for banter. In that almost pitch blackness, which was disorientating in itself, the dummies or projected images, popping out as if from nowhere, seemed to move even faster than usual. At times this made the men, even though seasoned troopers, forget that it was only an exercise and fire wildly, peppering the walls more than the targets. When this happened, they would nearly collapse with nervous exhaustion.

'You nearly shot *me* in there!' Carruthers bawled at Dymock. 'What the hell were you up to?'

'Sorry, Sarge, but it was so dark I just got confused and turned the wrong way. When you jumped up where the target should have been I fired automatically.'

'And nearly killed me!' Carruthers bawled.

'You shouldn't have been there,' Ainsworth told his fellow-sergeant. 'You turned the wrong way yourself and then jumped up right in front of the next target. We *all* nearly shot you!'

'That's not the point,' Carruthers said.

'What is?' Billings asked him.

'The point is to instantly judge the difference between the enemy and hostage, then shoot the right one. The fact that you bastards almost shot me just goes to show that you failed to differentiate between me and the target.'

'You shouldn't have been there,' Ainsworth insisted.

'That doesn't excuse you,' Carruthers replied. 'In a real CQB, in all the noise and confusion, men get scattered and can end up in the wrong place – but we still have to see who they are before we open fire. That's the whole bloody point of it.'

'We're just tired,' Dymock said. 'We've been doing too much of this. We've been doing it so much we've gone stale and that's the truth of the matter.'

'Freshen up,' Carruthers told him. 'And keep your bloody eyes open.'

When, after a few more weeks of this drill the men had still not been given further retraining in blasting metal locks off doors with Remington 870 pump-action shotguns or in acting as backup for each other in seizing locked rooms, they all guessed that whatever the forthcoming task, it would take place outdoors. They also guessed, from the fact that they were being trained in civilian clothing, that the mission was to be carried out in an area populated with civilians.

'Britain or overseas?' Dymock asked.

'Overseas,' Carruthers reckoned. 'And somewhere pretty warm. They're making us train in light, civilian clothing, which suggests a soft target in a warm climate.'

'What kind of soft target?' Billings asked.

'Non-military. That explains the civilian clothing. We're being prepared for a counter-terrorist mission in an area populated either entirely or largely by civilians.'

'At least it's not Belfast,' Ainsworth said. 'I've had enough of that hell-hole.'

'No, it won't be Belfast,' Carruthers told him. 'That much is certain. It's going to be overseas, somewhere warm, and where civilians gather.'

'Third World?' Ainsworth asked.

'I can't think of anywhere else where a CT mission would presently be required, so the Third World seems likely.'

'Some African shit-hole,' Dymock ventured. 'That would just be my luck. Malaria, rabies and AIDS. We've got a lot to look forward to!'

'It's time to get back to the Killing House,' Carruthers wearily reminded them.

'Lord have mercy!' Billings groaned.

'Not in the Killing House, he won't,' Dymock said.

Finally, after weeks of their tediously repetitive, nerve-racking, exhausting training, the four men were called to a briefing by the SAS Intelligence Corps, in a room in the 'Kremlin', the Operations Planning & Intelligence Wing. There they found Captain Edwards on the dais beside a senior 'green slime' officer who was, appropriately, wearing his green beret. Pinned to the board behind that unknown officer and Captain Edwards was a large, badly frayed and extensively annotated map of the Rock of Gibraltar.

8

The cold November winds were blowing even in Spain when the shadowy SAS Controller flew in with Alan Reid, a top Intelligence operator from the RUC's undercover surveillance team, F5, for a top-secret meeting with him and Chief Inspector José de Vega of the Málaga Special Branch regarding the presence of Sean Savage and Daniel McCann on Spanish soil. The Controller had been informed of the Irishmen's arrival in Spain by Madrid's Servicios de Información, the intelligence organization that had also arranged this visit to the Málaga Special Branch.

The movements of the two IRA members from Spain to Gibraltar and back to Ireland had led, over the past few months, to intense surveillance activity and cooperation between British and Spanish police, counter-terrorist and intelligence agencies. Now, having had lengthy discussions with his fellow 'green slime' officers in the SAS HQ in the Duke of York's Barracks, London, and agreed to general tactics in the event of a possible IRA attack on the Spanish mainland, or indeed Gibraltar, it was the Controller's intention to draft a counter-strategy with Spanish Intelligence and then quietly disappear from the scene, leaving the actual job of prevention to Captain Edwards and his four-man CRW team.

'It's our belief,' the Controller said, opening the conversation over coffee in a well-guarded room in the Málaga Special Branch building, 'that the changing of the guard outside the Governor of Gibraltar's residence is the terrorists' most likely target. By this I mean the changing of the guard and band parade ceremony of the 1st Battalion of the Royal Anglian Regiment, due to take place on 8 March 1988.'

'Yes. I agree. What better target could there be in terms of outrage?' Señor de Vega replied in perfect English.

'Quite,' the Controller said, not taking the situation as casually as his pragmatic Spanish friend. 'Our first step, therefore, was to postpone the ceremony, ostensibly for refurbishment of the guardhouse. The real reason, naturally, is to give our Intelligence services more time to prepare for the arrival of the terrorists when they plan the actual bombing.'

'Very wise,' Señor de Vega said. 'But when do you think that might be?'

'We don't know,' the Controller confessed, 'but we assume that when the same men, or other known or suspected terrorists, enter this country you'll inform us immediately.'

'Naturally. It is, after all, in our own interests. We cannot have such an outrage on Spanish soil – particularly as this is a British problem.'

'I appreciate that it isn't a Spanish problem, but we cannot prevent them from coming here. They're legally entitled to do so.'

'*We* could prevent them from coming into this country on the grounds that they're listed as known or suspected terrorists.'

'That remark,' the Controller said, 'is based on the assumption that the same people will return to do the bombing. That isn't necessarily so.'

'True,' Señor de Vega acknowledged. 'But even if they send others, we will almost certainly know – as you will – if they have terrorist links with those in Belfast. Most of these people, after all, even if not proven guilty of anything, are under surveillance – by us as well as by you. Our problem, therefore, irrespective of who comes here – and my personal belief is that the group will at least include the two who have already been here – is what to do when they arrive on Spanish soil.'

'On the assumption that the target is Gibraltar – and I think we can safely assume that it is – the problem taxing the British and Gibraltarian authorities is just when they should be detained.'

'Naturally we would detain them at the airport,' Señor de Vega said, looking a little puzzled, 'and return them instantly to Britain.'

The Controller did not reply immediately, looking a little uncomfortable. Finally, with what could have been a sigh, he said: 'Unfortunately we have a little problem with that.'

'A problem?'

'To move prematurely,' the Controller explained, obviously trying it on, 'would perhaps leave other IRA teams free to proceed with the bombing.'

'Other IRA teams?' Señor de Vega asked, even more confused by what was no more than a classic manoeuvre in the notorious repertoire of British diplomacy. 'Surely we would deal with those as they arrived – just as we would with the first group.'

At this point, Alan Reid, the softly spoken, politically adroit Intelligence operator from the RUC's undercover surveillance team, F5, coughed into his clenched fist, as if clearing his throat, and said: 'Please understand, Señor de Vega, that official Gibraltar is in a state of fear, if not actual panic, in the light of the recent events at Enniskillen.' He was referring to the bombing of 8 November, in the middle of the Remembrance Day parade in Enniskillen, in which sixty-three people had been wounded, some critically, and eleven people killed outright, including three married couples. 'Their fears,' he continued, 'have in no way been eased by the recent bomb attacks at the British headquarters of Rheindahlen in Germany and elsewhere. Official Gibraltar is frightened.'

'This is not Gibraltar,' Señor de Vega responded testily. 'This is Spain. So what is your point, Mr Reid?'

'My point, señor,' Reid replied in his soft Ulster accent, 'is that while the security people here in Spain are admirably cooperative, there's no guarantee that the Spanish courts will be willing to hand over terrorists to a government they don't really recognize.'

'You mean the government of Gibraltar.'

'Exactly. Nor will they hand the terrorists over to a UK which depends on a case of conspiracy as grounds for extradition.'

Señor de Vega, not a man to be won over by soft talk, yet understanding the need for warm relationships between Spain and Britain, thought about Reid's comments for a moment, then said: 'Naturally we're prepared to treat this affair as a perfectly legitimate surveillance of suspected international terrorists in transit through our jurisdiction.' He paused deliberately for dramatic effect, then added: 'So long as no one is likely to detonate any Semtex on Spanish territory.'

'In other words?' Reid asked.

'In other words, we must insist that any action taken against these terrorists must be taken on the Gibraltar side of the border.'

'In that case,' Mr Reid said smoothly, realizing that he was getting just what he and the Controller had wanted, 'the terrorists must be allowed into Gibraltar before any action against them is taken.'

'Exactly,' the Controller said, seeing instantly what the RUC Intelligence officer had done and so moving in to lend him support. 'The best place to arrest the terrorists will be on the road to Spain, where it crosses the Gibraltar airport runway. We can then bundle them aboard an aircraft and fly them straight back to Britain, secure in the knowledge that we've not only caught them, but done so publicly and gained ourselves a propaganda victory.'

'Which means,' said Señor de Vega, no longer confused but increasingly nervous, 'letting the terrorists pass through Málaga passport control and travel without interference from there to Gibraltar – a journey ninety per cent of which is through Spanish territory.'

A collective sigh signalled that this was, unfortunately, the case.

'We will, of course, provide you with names and photos,' Mr Reid said in a thoughtful manner, 'to ensure that you know just who you're dealing with and enable you to track them throughout their journey. Knowing exactly who they are will also enable you to intervene at any juncture where you feel they may be about to commit an offence on Spanish soil.'

'Most kind of you,' Señor de Vega said with all the dry aplomb of David Niven.

After thinking about the proposal for some time, the Spaniard, who was as politically adroit as the Ulsterman, said: 'This is all very well and good, Mr Reid, but what makes you so sure that the bombing will take place in Gibraltar and not on Spanish soil?'

Reid smiled, acknowledging that he realized he was not dealing with a fool. 'Soon after the IRA's bombing of the

Remembrance Day parade at Enniskillen on 8 November,' he said, 'British signallers in Gibraltar detected a powerful radio tone transmitted on a military frequency. Though the exact source remains unclear, that transmission was traced to the Spanish mainland. As British security is presently engaged in the most secret of secret wars against terrorism – the war of electronics – this mysterious transmission naturally has them worried.'

'This I understand,' Señor de Vega replied. 'It's a well-known fact that, with the help of technology supplied by American citizens and institutions as well as revolutionary regimes such as Libya, the IRA, now the oldest terrorist group in the world, has also become the most innovative. In fact, with regard to modern technology, it is highly advanced.'

'Exactly what I'm saying,' Mr Reid concurred.

'So how does this relate to the Enniskillen atrocity?'

'The Enniskillen bomb was detonated by a simple timer. It was, in effect, a form of targeting based on blind and indiscriminate guesswork. However, the IRA can do better than that when it so desires.'

'Meaning?'

'More precise operations,' the SAS Controller informed him at a nod from Mr Reid, 'already tended to use a bomb that exploded in response to a signal from a human observer, whether by a command wire leading to a device concealed in a culvert or hedge or – as in the assassination of Lord Mountbatten off the Irish coast in 1979, or the Lord Chief Justice of Appeal for Northern Ireland on the Irish border in 1987 – by radio signal. Indeed, hard as it is to believe, some of the IRA's signal equipment was adapted from such innocent artefacts as model aircraft.'

'I believe it,' Señor de Vega said. 'But where is this leading us?'

'Our most recent countermeasures designed to jam the bombers' systems,' the Controller confessed, 'have encountered three new problems. One is that the terrorists are known to be working to adapt American radar equipment, normally used for detecting speeding motorists, to trigger bombs, but operating on much higher frequencies – say, 10,000 megahertz and above.'

'Such as?'

'To give you an example: wallet-sized radar sensors costing about £75 and rewired for use as detonators are often concealed in target vehicles. To set off the charge, an electronic gun normally used by police in estimating a car's speed can be aimed at the target from a distance of half a mile. When the signal's detected by the radar receiver, the bomb explodes.'

'Very neat,' Señor de Vega commented drily.

'Another refinement,' Reid said, wishing to add his contribution to the seduction of the wary Spanish Intelligence officer, 'has been described by Dr Michael Scott, a lecturer in electronics at the National Institute for Higher Education in Dublin.' Ignoring Señor de Vega's raised eyebrows, he continued: 'Having noted that each side in Ireland is involved in what he described as a race to produce and counter new technology, a survival of the technologically fittest, he pointed out that a method favoured by the IRA is a hybrid device linking a mechanical clock, such as the timer from a parking meter, to an electrical contact. This prevents the radio signal from working until a certain time has passed – and it is, according to Dr Scott, an absolutely fail-safe way of stopping a signal getting through before the man with the button is ready.'

Señor de Vega sighed. 'All of this is very impressive, but it still doesn't persuade me that the target will be Gibraltar, rather than Spain.'

'The third nightmare haunting Gibraltar,' the Controller informed him, 'is that the mysterious signal intercepted shortly after the Enniskillen bombing in November was not inter- preted as a means of detonating a bomb but of priming it in such a way that the next signal on the same military frequency – probably from an Army vehicle in the immediate vicinity, engaged in routine signals traffic – would cause the explosion. This means, in short, that whatever the precise design of the bomb to be planted by the IRA in Gibraltar, it is our consid- ered opinion that it could be triggered by radio from anywhere in Spain.'

'The fact that it *could* be triggered from Spain doesn't mean that it *will* be,' said Señor de Vega, a stubborn man. 'More likely, if they wish to bomb Gibraltar, they will trigger the bomb from there.'

'No,' the Controller said firmly. 'We don't think so. According to the Royal Signals team on Gibraltar who analysed the transmissions from Spain, the signal appeared to become stronger as they drove towards the Spanish border on the landward side of the colony's airport, farthest away from the Rock. In other words, the terrorists appear to be planning to allay all suspicions regarding their presence on the Rock by planting the bomb there, then exploding it at a later time, or even date, from somewhere in Spain – most likely La Línea, right on the border, though possibly farther away.'

'What precisely are you trying to tell me?' Señor de Vega asked.

'Rightly or wrongly, we're basing our plans on three assumptions,' the Controller told him. 'One: that there's a plot to place a car bomb somewhere in Gibraltar. Two: that the bomb will be detonated by a radio or radar pulse, possibly on a military frequency. Three: that the terrorists might be able to detonate the weapon from the sanctuary of foreign territory; in this case, on the Spanish side of the Spanish-Gibraltar border. For this reason we need your help in intercepting – and possibly neutralizing – the terrorists before that bomb is exploded. Will you give it?'

'Have I a choice?' the Spaniard asked.

'No,' the Controller said.

Señor de Vega glanced from the Controller to the gently smiling RUC Intelligence officer, then raised his hands in the air as if offering a prayer.

'What is a poor man to do,' he asked, 'when he is given no choice? Yes, gentlemen, Spain will cooperate. We will keep our eye on your terrorists. Now may I offer you cognac?'

'Please do,' the Controller said.

9

The sky was hanging low and slate-grey over Belfast when, in late February 1988, Pat Tyrone paid a visit to Mairead at the small house in Andersonstown where she was then living. Not expecting him, Mairead was sitting in front of an open fire in the cramped living-room, holding in her cold hands a cup of hot tea laced with whisky.

She felt like death. She always did these days. Ever since the death of Tom, killed by his own bomb, she had felt that she had somehow lost herself and was empty inside. Mairead rarely went out now, but instead spent most of her days either lying in bed in a daze or sitting in her chair, either watching television or simply staring into the fire. She found it very hard to read; her concentration was completely gone. When she picked up a book, the words blurred before her eyes and she started thinking of Tom, seeing his face before her, practically feeling him, desperately wanting to hold him and be held by him, until reality clamped around her again and she filled up with pain. That pain was like a cancer inside her, blotting out all reasonable thought. She wanted to die and be with him.

The doorbell rang. Not hearing it at first, lost in her dead world, Mairead continued sipping her hot tea. Eventually, however, the insistent ringing pierced her consciousness. Placing the teacup on the mantelpiece, above the blazing fire, she went to open the front door. She was still wearing only her dressing-gown but she didn't care about that. Opening the door, she was surprised to find Pat Tyrone smiling at her, though his grey gaze was searching.

'Surprised to see me?' he asked her.

'Yes.'

'How have you been, Mairead?'

'Ach, all right, I suppose.'

'Maureen tells me you haven't been well.'

'Sure, I'm all right. I'm fine. I just don't go out much.'

'Aye, it must be hard for you . . . I mean Tom an' all.'

'I'm over that,' Mairead lied. 'What do you want, Pat?'

Tyrone glanced to both sides, keeping his eye on the soldiers at the checkpoints at both ends of the street, then he turned back to Mairead. 'Can I come in?'

She stared thoughtfully at him for a moment, then shrugged. 'Sure, why not?' she said. When he had stepped inside, she indicated the other chair in front of the blazing fire. 'Can I get you a cup of tea?' she asked. Tyrone shook his head, and Mairead returned to the chair she had been sitting in, asking once again as she sat down: 'So what do you want?'

'Sure, that doesn't sound too friendly,' Tyrone said teasingly.

Mairead managed a smile. 'I'm not bein' unfriendly,' she told him. 'I just want to know why you're here.'

'I'm here to see how you feel.'

'You must know how I feel. I'm not really recovered. I'll never recover. When Tom died, so did I.'

'That's melodramatic, Mairead.'

'It's a fact of life, Pat. I've lost my heart and soul, lost my strength, an ' now I just watch the days pass. I feel empty inside.'

'You need to do something.'

'You're tryin' to get me back to work.'

'Why not? It'd be better than just sittin' here, day in, day out.'

'I like sittin' here.'

'No, you don't. You just do it because you've lost the will to live, but that can't go on for ever.'

'Like to bet on it?'

'No, Mairead, I wouldn't. But we need you. And you need us. That's why I'm here. We have a job for you, and I think it would do you good to get involved. You need to force yourself out of here.'

'I want nothin' that reminds me of Tom.'

'Everything will remind you of Tom, so that's no excuse, Mairead. Sure, every time you switch on the telly, you'll see news of the Troubles and think of Tom. Every time you read about a bombin', you think about Tom. Every time you step out on that street and see a Brit soldier, you'll be thinkin' of Tom. Until you fill your life with somethin' else, you'll always think about Tom. We think about him as well; he was one of our best men. We think about him, but that doesn't stop us: we just keep on with the work. So do this job for us, Mairead – and do it for yourself. It'll get you out of this house and also take you out of yourself and help you stop all this broodin'. Believe me, it will.'

Mairead gazed into the flickering yellow flames and saw them constantly changing shape, forming figures and faces. She saw Tom there, felt the burning in her soul, and realized that though Tyrone was exploiting her, he was right in what he had said. She couldn't live this way for ever and the time had come to change things. Besides, as she really wanted to die, why not go back to work? She might find death through it.

'What's the job?' she asked.

Pleased, Tyrone told her about Gibraltar, then summarized the task: 'We've decided that the best time and place for the bombing would be the band assembly area during the changing of the guard and band parade ceremony of the 1st Battalion of the Royal Anglian Regiment, when there should be lots of tourists about. The ceremony's scheduled to take place on 8 March. That means we have time to check out the area more thoroughly than Sean and Mad Dan did. We want you to do that.'

'You want me to go to Gibraltar?'

'Aye. Via Spain. Like Sean and Mad Dan, you'll go just like a normal tourist and make your own way down to the Rock. Lots of tourists do it: they cross over to the Rock, have a good look around or do a bit of duty-free shopping, then return to Spain the same day. That's what you'll do, like. Except you'll do it more than once – at least as many times as is required to suss out the whole area and decide the best way to insert the bomb. Sure, you'll also pick up a suntan, which can't be that bad.'

Mairead actually smiled, then brushed her long hair back from her pale face. 'Who's to do the actual bombing?'

'You, Sean and Mad Dan. We think that'd be best because you're the three that are goin' to know the place and how to move around it. Will you do it?'

Mairead studied the flickering flames in the fire, seeing images, ghosts, the face of someone she'd loved. The pain that now resided in the heart of her welled up like a flood and she had to escape that. Tom had died bombing the hated Brits, so in a sense they had caused his death. Mairead hadn't really hated the Brits before – they were just the enemy – but so many of those she loved had died in the war against them and now Mairead hated them. On the other hand, the very thought of having anything to do with Mad Dan . . .

'Why Mad Dan?' she asked.

'Why not?'

'He has the reputation of being a mad dog who enjoys the killin'. I don't think I'd like that.'

'He may be that, all right, but he's also a good man to have in a tight spot and one who knows all about plantin' bombs. In fact, no matter what he's like personally, he's one of our best.'

'I'd rather go with someone else.'

'You like Sean, all right?'

'Ackaye, he's a good wee lad. Sure, I like him a lot.'

'Then let him be your comfort. He'll act as a balancer. Just stick close to him and try not to take too much notice of anything Mad Dan says – other than anything relatin' to the mission, that is. He knows his business that way. Now will you do it or not?'

Mairead thought about it for some time, gradually accepting that she needed such a job to stop her from brooding and becoming more melancholic.

'Yes,' she said, hoping to sweep the pain away with the strength of her hatred. 'I'll do it. When do I leave?'

'In a few days,' Tyrone told her. 'You'll travel under two different passports, flying Aer Lingus from Dublin to Brussels as Mary Johnston, and from there to Málaga with a stolen British passport in the name of Mrs Katherine Alison Smith. You'll be booked into a hotel in Marbella – just another tourist, like, in an upmarket area – and from there you can make a few day trips to Gibraltar, taking normal tourist buses. Once on the Rock, you can wander about at your leisure, taking in all the sights. No one'll suspect a thing, even if you take photographs, which we want you to do. We want you to reconnoitre the whole area and come back here with a game plan. So pack your suitcase, include some summery clothes, and I'll come back tomorrow with the tickets and passports. Thanks a lot, Mairead.'

'No need for thanks,' Mairead said. 'I'm doin' this for myself. I see nothin' in my future but another spell in prison or an early grave. I just hope it's the latter.'

Tyrone stood up and placed his hand on her shoulder, shaking her affectionately. 'You're just down at the moment, Mairead, but sure you'll feel better soon – when you get to Gibraltar. Apart from the sunshine, you'll feel a lot better knowing that you're doin' something for the cause. Till tomorrow, then.'

'Right.'

Mairead stayed in the chair, studying the flames, as Tyrone let himself out. Sitting there, she smiled slightly, bitterly, then sighed and nodded off.

Three days later, carrying two false passports in her shoulder bag and dressed like a smart businesswoman, Mairead caught the train from Belfast to Dublin. Not wishing to draw attention to herself, she buried her nose in a book until the train reached Dublin, where she picked up a bus to the airport. After checking in at the Aer Lingus desk, she passed through customs using the false passport in the name of Mary Johnston. No questions were asked.

Again, Mairead managed to avoid conversation by concentrating on her book while having a drink in the bar of the departure lounge. In the plane to Brussels, however, she was seated beside an English businessman who first kept glancing sideways at her, clearly smitten by her pale beauty and long, black hair, and finally, when the steward came along with the drinks trolley, ordered a white wine for himself and asked if Mairead would like a drink too.

'Sure, that would be grand,' Mairead replied, realizing that conversation was inevitable and deciding to get something out of it. 'I'll have a wee whisky, thanks.'

'Irish!' the man exclaimed softly as the drinks were being served. 'I should have known by the looks of you.'

'Oh, how?'

'That long, dark hair. The pale skin. Just something about you.'

Mairead smiled cynically, knowing he was talking shite and hadn't known she was Irish until she opened her mouth. 'Aye, I suppose so.'

'Ken Chambers,' the man said, introducing himself.

'Mary Johnston. Nice to meet you.'

'I've been to Ireland a lot,' Chambers said when the steward had served the drinks and moved on. 'North *and* south. The people on both sides are so pleasant, it's hard to believe what goes on there . . . all the bombings, the shootings, kneecappings. It hardly makes sense.'

'Nor to me,' Mairead lied, enjoying her whisky. 'It's just one of those things, like.'

'Bad to live there, is it?'

'Desperate,' Mairead said, pushing the long hair back from her face and sipping more whisky. 'But you get used to it, don't you? Like you Brits did during the Blitz. It becomes natural, like.'

'Yes, I suppose so,' Chambers said. 'Are you going to Brussels on business?'

'No,' Mairead replied. 'Just the transit lounge. I'm on my way to Spain and got a cheap flight by going this way. I'm off to pick up a suntan.'

'Oh,' Chambers said, obviously disappointed, having imagined he was on to a good thing, 'what a pity. I know an awful lot about Brussels, I could have shown you round.'

'Too bad,' Mairead said.

Though not hiding his disappointment, Chambers remained pleasant enough and made small talk throughout the rest of the flight. When the aircraft had landed at Brussels, he waved goodbye and headed for passport control while Mairead went straight to the transit lounge. As she did not have to show her passport here and would go through Málaga airport using the other false passport, there would be no record of a Mary Johnston having disembarked at either Brussels or Málaga. Mary Johnston, in a sense, already no longer existed and Mairead would pass through Málaga under the name of Mrs Katherine Alison Smith.

The flight was uneventful. Mairead had a window seat beside a rather formal, middle-aged couple who rarely talked to each other and, in the case of the woman, who was in the middle seat, only offering the most basic, distracted pleasantries to Mairead when passing her the food tray or miniature bottles of whisky.

Mairead had three whiskies in quick succession and became pleasantly, though imperceptibly drunk. In fact, by now she was really feeling like a tourist and almost enjoying herself. It was only when she thought of her dead lover that the pain returned to torment her.

But she was thrilled to see the parched, mountainous landscape of southern Spain spread out below her, crisscrossed with snaking rivers, dotted here and there with brown-roofed, white houses, some isolated on the hillsides, others clustered together as villages and towns. Even though it was November the sun was shining over the land as brightly as during an Irish summer. She felt better already.

A fleeting moment of panic came when she had to pass through passport control, but the Spanish official scarcely glanced at the second false passport, merely noting that it was an old-fashioned British one and waving her through. The customs officers didn't even check her suitcase and soon she was outside.

As instructed by Tyrone, she took a cab to her hotel in Estepona. She thought the views along the coastline were wonderful, but she was puritanically shocked by how long the journey was and how much it cost. Nevertheless, she had been given the money to cover it, so she paid, overtipping the delighted driver, and then entered the hotel

The receptionist spoke English, which made checking in easy, and soon Mairead was sitting in a rattan chair on the balcony of her room, drinking another whisky and gazing across the road to the vast, glittering Mediterranean. It was nice to go travelling.

She had the first good night's sleep she'd had in a long time and woke the next morning feeling particularly refreshed. Dazzled by the brilliance of the light, she put on light clothing – shirt, cotton slacks and flat shoes – and went down for breakfast. She felt self-conscious in the dining-room, too aware of the fact that she was being stared at surreptitiously by the other guests. One reason was simply that she was a woman holidaying alone; the other that she was a strikingly attractive woman with long, lustrous hair.

Finishing breakfast, which was standard British fare for the tourists – bacon and eggs, toast and coffee – she went down to the lobby and checked the notice-board, where she found leaflets advertising day trips to Gibraltar. Seeing that she was still early enough to pick up the last of the trips, she bought a ticket and hurried out to the bus, which, minutes later, was trundling along the busy, scenic N340, *en route* to the Spanish-Gibraltar border at La Línea.

Once more, Mairead was thrilled by the scenery on either side of the road, which snaked sinuously between the sierras and the green-blue Mediterranean, all under a vast azure sky with few clouds. Normally oppressed by the low, grey skies of Northern Ireland, Mairead now felt that she was spreading her wings, as free as a bird.

'Fantastic, isn't it?' the portly woman seated beside her said.

'Ackaye,' Mairead replied. 'Sure, I've never seen anything like it. My eyes hurt just to look at it.'

'Irish?'

'Wouldn't you know it?'

'Never been here before?'

'No.'

'Then it must be quite a contrast from home – I mean all of this sunshine.'

'Sure, it is, right enough.'

'Here on holiday?'

'Aye.'

'On your own?'

'Aye.'

'That makes two of us,' the Englishwoman said. 'You're all right on your own here.'

'You've come before?' Mairead asked.

'Every year,' the woman said. 'I came with my husband every year for fifteen years, but he died four years ago. I still come. I pretend he's beside me. I still love it here.'

Mairead thought about Tom and the scalding pain returned. 'I understand why you do,' she said quickly, not wanting to show her emotions. 'Sure, it's real lovely here. I might come back myself. Just look at that sea and sky!'

However, once at the border, which was a surprisingly unattractive area, she was reminded again of Belfast and her dead lover. With the brutally swift return of her grief and pain, she forced herself to think of just why she was there and disembarked from the bus on the Spanish side of the border in order to walk the rest of the way and see as much as possible.

'I know this place so well,' the woman said. 'Let me show you around.'

'Sure, that's kind of you,' Mairead told her, 'but I'd like to walk the whole way, rather than taking the bus.'

'Fine. I don't mind,' the woman said, smiling broadly. 'You always see more on foot, so we'll walk and talk.'

'Really, you don't have to.'

'Honestly, I don't mind.'

'Sure, I'd really prefer to be on my own and keep my own thoughts, like.'

'Oh, nonsense!' the woman said.

Suddenly exasperated, hardly thinking of what she was doing, Mairead shoved her face close to the other woman and whispered fiercely: 'Do I have to say it half a dozen times to make myself understood? I want to be alone, you stupid cow, so get back on that bus.'

'Well, I never . . .'

When Mairead jabbed her finger at the bus, the shocked woman beat a hasty retreat and clambered up into it. Relieved, Mairead turned away and walked towards the airport. 'Dumb bitch,' she hissed.

After crossing the runway, she walked along Winston Churchill Avenue, passing a petrol station. A short distance farther on, coming to the junction of Smith Darrien Road and Corral Road, she took the latter and walked all the way down to Main Street and the central shopping area. She didn't even have to ask to find the band assembly area, as the guards on duty were enough to tell her where she was. Once there, however, she walked around, gawping and taking photographs just like all the other tourists, but paying particular attention to what surrounded the assembly area.

The Hambros Bank, she noted, was directly opposite the assembly area, just across Line Wall Road, and the Garrison Theatre was right beside it, where the road turned back towards the border at the public car park by the High Stone Wall. That same route, Mairead soon found out after asking a few questions at a nearby pub, was also the route taken by the parade after the band of the 1st Battalion of the Royal Anglian Regiment had assembled. Just down from the bank was the Jewish Old People's Home. Behind the High Stone Wall was the Toc-H Hostel and the Bishop Fitzgerald School. Apart from the high density of buildings around the assembly area, it was a real little corner of England packed with shoppers and tourists: men, women and children.

In terms of casualties designed to cause public outrage, it could not have been bettered.

Mairead, who had suffered the pain of loss, tried not to think of the dreadful pain she would cause to others if she set a bomb off here. The end justifies the means, she told herself.

Having taken all the photos she required, she went to the pub she had been to earlier and there, over a pint of Guinness, she made a drawing of the area, with arrows indicating how her comrades could enter the area, deposit the bomb and then leave before it exploded. She also meticulously noted the exact location of the car park where, as she would recommend, a 'blocking' car could be left for two or three days before the car bringing in the bomb took its place, just before the timed explosion.

Satisfied with her work, and noting that it was already late afternoon, Mairead walked back across the runway and boarded the bus that would take her back to Estepona.

She slept well that night and returned to Gibraltar the following day, this time to observe with other tourists the routine changing of the guard and then follow the route that would be taken by the bandsmen during the major band ceremony on 8 March.

She did this every day for the rest of the week, always taking photographs and jotting down many notes, and by the end of the week had worked out that between 130 and 145lb of Semtex, appropriately located, would devastate this densely packed area during the band ceremony, and that a retaliation highly successful in propaganda terms would thereby be realized.

By concentrating on words such as 'propaganda' and 'retaliation' she could forget words such as 'carnage'. She could thus, without feeling too much remorse, avenge Tom and all the other comrades who had died for the cause.

When she had completed her research, she phoned Pat Tyrone from the privacy of her hotel room and informed him: 'The job can be done. Sure, it should be right easy.'

'Good,' Tyrone replied. 'Then stay where you are and I'll arrange to have someone come and see you about getting enough groceries to keep you goin' until you have to come home.'

Tyrone was referring to the Irishman resident in the area who would visit her in the hotel regarding the supply of enough Semtex for the bombing.

'Fine,' Mairead replied. 'An' what about the help you promised me?' she asked, referring to Sean and Mad Dan.

'They'll fly out on 5 March. Sure, I'll fax you details of the flight and trust that you'll meet them at the airport.'

'Ackaye, I'll do that all right. It's the least I can do, like.'

'Enjoy yourself in the meantime. Do some more sightseein'. Have a good time.'

'Sure, it's nice to go travellin',' Mairead said.

'It's all part of the job,' Tyrone replied, then the line went dead.

Mairead replaced the receiver and walked on to the balcony of her room to look out at the sea, now turning grey in the dimming light of winter. Sitting down at the glass-topped table, she opened a romantic novel and started reading – simply passing the time until the Irishman arrived to negotiate the purchase of 145lb of Semtex.

Mairead had not passed through Gibraltar unobserved. Under surveillance in Belfast from the moment she had left prison in September 1986, she had been observed at every stop on the journey from Belfast to Málaga. Also, determined not to let international terrorism, Irish or otherwise, flex its muscles in Spain, the Servicios de Información in Madrid had given permission for a junior representative of the Gibraltarian Special Branch, Detective Constable Kenneth Wilby, to mount a special surveillance operation on the Spanish side of the border.

Seated in an enclosed room beside a Spanish immigration officer, Wilby was facing a screen on to which the Spaniards projected images of passport photographs and numbers taken from people crossing the border. Car registration numbers were also passed to him by the Spanish immigration officer, who was in contact by telephone with his colleagues watching the cars go through.

As both the British and Spanish authorities knew about the visit of two suspected terrorists the previous November, as well as Mairead's arrival in Málaga airport just a few days ago, Wilby had been instructed to look out for two men and a woman travelling either together, or seperately, from Ireland under false passports, but already included in the photographic files of the passport and border security officers concerned with international terrorism.

Mairead was therefore identified by Detective Constable Wilby when she crossed the border from Spain into Gibraltar. Nevertheless, when he saw her entering Gibraltar, as instructed he made no attempt to stop her. Instead, he kept checking, hoping to see the two men. When they failed to materialize, Wilby merely logged the time of Mairead's return to the border as she crossed back into Spain. He did this meticulously every day, still not interfering with her movements, because, as he had been informed, the Spanish and British authorities had jointly decided not to act until it was clear that a terrorist outrage was being prepared – which would most likely be when all three terrorists had entered Gibraltar together.

In short, they would not be stopped from entering Gibraltar, with or without their car and its possible bomb. They would, however, be stopped, either by arrest or by lethal gunshots, once they were all in Gibraltar.

10

'A bombing is definitely imminent,' the Controller said, opening the meeting of the Joint Intelligence Committee in London. 'We can now confirm that the trip of two well-known IRA members, Sean Savage and Daniel McCann, to Spain and Gibraltar, has been followed up with a separate trip by Mairead Farrell, the woman who bombed a Loyalist hotel in Belfast a decade ago, spent the next ten years in prison, and then, on her release, became intimately involved with Tom Riley, who was killed by his own bomb last year when he tried to blow up another Protestant hotel. Farrell therefore has to be treated as a known terrorist who, when she went to Spain nine days ago, visited Gibraltar five days in a row and was observed doing so by the Gibraltarian Special Branch. We can only deduce from this that the target is definitely Gibraltar.'

There was an uneasy silence for a moment, broken only when the Secretary asked: 'Whereabouts on Gibraltar?'

The Controller sighed with relief, realizing that he would now have the Secretary's fullest cooperation. 'While we can't yet be sure, we think the most likely target will be an assembly point where the band of the garrison regiment, the 1st

129

Battalion of the Royal Anglian Regiment, prepares for the ceremonial parade – the Changing of the Guard. This takes place in what's actually a public thoroughfare surrounded by buildings including houses, shops, a theatre, an old people's home and, worst of all with regard to potential casualties, a school.'

The Secretary visibly winced at the last named. 'Dreadful,' he murmured.

'Naturally,' the Controller added, 'during the Changing of the Guard the place fills up with tourists, who would also become victims of such a bomb.'

'Do we know the identities of the bomb team?'

'We don't yet know just who will arrive in Gibraltar or when,' the leader of the Special Military Intelligence Unit replied. 'But the Spanish authorities have confirmed that the two men who passed through Málaga airport under false passports last November were Sean Savage and Daniel McCann, both known terrorists under constant surveillance. Savage is twenty-three and a young man of many hobbies, including rambling, cycling, football, cooking and the Irish language. He doesn't smoke or drink and has never publicly expressed a political viewpoint. In fact, few of those who know him would believe that he's in the IRA. Nevertheless, he is. Though his IRA involvement is strictly covert, we know for a fact that he's an expert engineer, or bomb maker, responsible for more than one atrocity.'

'And McCann?' the Secretary asked.

'A thirty-year-old butcher's assistant from the Clonnard district of Belfast, known far and wide as "Mad Dan". Began his IRA activities at the age of twelve, in the summer of 1969, shortly after Catholic homes in his district were burnt to the ground by the Loyalists. The remarkable thing is that in the many years he's been an IRA assassin he's only been convicted once for anything major. He got two years in the Maze for possessing a detonator. As the name suggests, Mad Dan's the kind of fanatical activist who knows no compromise and implacably opposes what he sees as Britain's criminal presence in his country. The RUC regarded him as a particularly ruthless exponent of shoot-to-kill. Indeed, they hold him responsible for the murders of Detective Sergeants Michael Malone and Ernest Carson in August last year. They were off duty, taking a glass in a part of Belfast traditionally regarded as neutral ground. Having murdered Malone and Carson and wounded another police officer and a barman, McCann fled in a waiting car.'

'I take it,' the Secretary said in his dry manner, 'that you feel the world would be a better place without him.'

'I do, sir.'

'And we're absolutely sure that he and this Sean Savage were in Spain last November?'

'Absolutely. Savage told his mother that he was taking a break in Galway. Instead, he . . .'

'How do you know what he said to his mother?'

'He's been under surveillance for the past eighteen months. During a deliberately mounted cordon-and-search sweep of the area, when the residents of Savage's street were temporarily evicted from their homes, one of our surveillance teams entered his house and inserted a miniature fibre-optic probe on top of the picture-rail running around the living-room. That probe was tuned to an advanced laser audio-surveillance transceiver that picked up all conversations taking place inside the room. So we were able to record Savage telling his mother that he was taking a break in Galway when in fact he went to Dublin – we had him under visual surveillance by now – and from there flew to Málaga via Gatwick, with a driving licence, birth and baptism certificate and organ-donor card in the name of Brendan Coyne. McCann travelled separately, also with false documentation, as Robert Wilfred Reilly. The two men met at Málaga airport, hired a white Renault 5 from Avis, and then spent the next seven days travelling along the N340 from Málaga to Algeciras, and crossed at least once into Gibraltar.'

'They were observed entering Gibraltar?'

'Yes. Covertly photographed and entered in the records by the Gibraltarian Special Branch in cooperation with the Spanish police on the Spanish side of the border.'

'How long were they in Spain?'

'Seven days.'

'Did they meet anyone there?'

'They did a lot of drinking – at least McCann did – in a lot of bars, particularly Irish pubs, where doubtless they picked up information from innocent locals. They may also have had arranged meetings with fellow-terrorists, or the suppliers of explosives, but we can't be sure of this as the Spanish police lost them for long periods of time, notably during their trips along the N340.'

'And now we have this female entering the picture, following in their tracks.'

'Yes, Mr Secretary. Though a former convent school girl from Andersonstown, Mairead Farrell is a woman with particularly strong – and possibly deadly – motivation.'

'How come?'

'After leaving the convent school, she served ten years in prison, most of them in Armagh, for planting a bomb in a Loyalist hotel in Belfast in 1976. According to our informants, those ten years merely strengthened her resolve and made her a more fanatical IRA activist. Nevertheless, she appears to have ceased her political activities since getting out of prison in September 1986.'

'So why would you think of her as still being highly motivated?'

'Because last November, just before Savage and McCann arrived in Málaga, Mairead's lover and fellow-bomber, Tom Riley – a man suspected of some very important assassinations, as well as numerous bombings – blew himself up accidentally when bombing a Protestant hotel in Belfast. That same evening, a pub frequented by Provisional IRA leader Patrick Tyrone was under SAS surveillance from a loft in the house opposite and Mairead was observed entering that pub just before the explosion of the bomb that killed her lover. Shortly after the bomb went off, a visibly disturbed Tyrone entered the pub. He emerged with his wife and a sobbing Mairead Farrell. A short time later, Farrell showed up in Málaga. Though recognized instantly as a known terrorist from the photo files held by the Spanish security police at Malaga's passport control, she was travelling with a false passport in the name of Mrs Katherine Alison Smith. Also, she had flown in from Brussels via Dublin – an unnecessarily elaborate route to take and one clearly designed to make her hard to track.'

'But the Spanish police let her through without attempting to arrest her or even question her.'

'At our request, yes. We saw little point in stopping her and we really wanted to know what she was up to.'

'Gibraltar.'

'Yes. It's our belief that Patrick Tyrone used the death of Tom Riley to encourage Farrell back into the business, perhaps as an act of vengeance against the Brits. Subsequently she visited Gibraltar five days in a row. As a known bomber, we believe she's there to reconnoitre the area and plan a forthcoming attack – almost certainly near the band assembly area during the band ceremony planned for 8 March.'

'Like the first two, this woman was *definitely* observed entering Gibraltar?'

'Yes, Mr Secretary. Exactly like the other two, she was photographed and listed entering and leaving the Rock by the local Special Branch acting with the Spanish police on their side of the border.'

There was a moment's tense silence, then the SMIU leader said: 'I don't think I have to tell anyone around this table what a bomb explosion in such a densely packed area, particularly during such a ceremony, would do in terms of human and political devastation. We simply cannot let that happen.'

After another long silence, during which the men glanced uneasily at one another and the Secretary thoughtfully scratched his nose, the latter finally said: 'I agree. So what happens now?'

The Controller coughed into his clenched fist. 'We notify the Joint Operations Centre – which includes an SAS liaison officer – to dispatch an SAS Special Projects Team of a dozen men to Gibraltar, along with a number of security people of both sexes, mainly from MI5, augmented by local Special Branch personnel, to act as watchers and an armed reserve. This operation will be code-named "Flavius".'

'Was that name chosen for a particular reason?' the Secretary asked.

The Controller smiled. 'Whatever can you mean, Mr Secretary?'

'I did ancient history at Cambridge and, as I recall, Flavius was a Roman magistrate who enforced the rule of law. His role model was a Roman soldier of common background, grandson of a gladiator and a centurion, who fought his way to the top, was eventually hailed as the Emperor Vespasian in AD 69, and took over a Rome debauched by the excesses of the mad Emperor Nero. A year later, Vespasian opened the Flavian Amphitheatre, otherwise known as the Colosseum, which became the place where public duels between gladiators were held.'

Still smiling, the Controller said: 'I don't see what you're driving at. I . . .'

'Flavius's circus specialized in the type of combat with no rules except that the winner is the man who walks away alive. Is that the game plan for Gibraltar?'

The Controller thought a moment before answering, then decided on honesty. 'The aim of the operation is arrest – arrest, disarm, defuse the bomb. But we have to bear in mind that we're going after dedicated terrorists, an Active Service Unit who're planning to explode a bomb in a crowded public place and may do so by using a remote-control device triggered by a button on their person. We have to ensure, when we tackle them, that none of them presses that button. That doesn't leave any time for indecision. So, yes, if the terrorists cannot be arrested, or if they refuse to surrender – if, in other words, it gets to a fire-fight – we will shoot to kill.'

'I understand,' the Secretary said. 'Operation Flavius is hereby authorized. You may proceed at will, gentlemen.'

The meeting was adjourned and the Controller hurried back to SAS HQ at the Duke of York's Barracks, to get in touch with his Special Projects Team and prepare them for Gibraltar.

Operation Flavius was under way.

11

Before his second trip to Spain, Sean told his mother that he was taking another holiday across the border, staying in a caravan and studying the language. But once again he took the train to Dublin and flew to Málaga, this time via Paris, with the same false papers in the name of Brendan Coyne. He arrived in Málaga at 8.50 p.m. on Friday 4 March on the same Iberia flight as 'Robert Wilfred Reilly' – actually Daniel McCann.

Mairead met both men at the airport and led them out to the white Renault 5 she had hired the day before. She had always liked Sean, who she thought was rather sensitive and killed only with reluctance, but she detested Mad Dan and fully understood why he had that nickname. McCann was a mad dog, efficient when it came to the gun, but not trustworthy otherwise. She knew why he'd been chosen for this task, but she still didn't like it.

'Sure, I've actually hired two cars,' she told them. 'The other's the same as this one – a white Renault 5. One's to take us to the Rock and be used as a blockin' car; the other's to transport the bomb the next day, driven by someone else.'

'Who?' Mad Dan asked testily.

'You're not to know that,' Mairead told him. 'Pat Tyrone was adamant about that. He said the less each of us knew the better it'd be for the movement if we were caught by the Brits.'

'Sure, isn't it quare good to know how confident he is in us?' Mad Dan said, practically sneering. 'Caught by the Brits, like.'

'Confidence breeds mistakes,' Mairead told him. 'Tyrone has it right.'

Having placed their travelling bags in the boot of the Renault, the two men clambered into the car, Sean in the back and Mad Dan beside Mairead, who was driving.

'I hate drivin' on this side of the road,' she said. 'It makes me feel really nervous.'

'Ackaye,' Sean said candidly. 'I felt exactly the same. Sure, I hardly knew my left side from my right, but I managed it somehow. You get used to it, don't you?'

'Aye, you do, but I'm still feelin' nervous.'

'So we're actually goin' to do it,' Sean said as Mairead turned out on to the N340, heading westwards into the brilliant March light with the Mediterranean glittering on the left, beyond the white houses, blue sea meeting blue sky in the horizon's heat haze.

'I don't know yet,' Mairead surprised herself by saying. 'We're goin' out to have another look at the place, but I still have my doubts.'

'That's not what you told Tyrone,' Mad Dan said. 'He said *you* said the target was perfect.'

'Aye, it is in certain ways. But I've had growing doubts about certain aspects of it an' I'm thinkin' more an' more about those. Maybe it's just bein' out here on my own. Sure, we'll know soon enough.'

'What doubts?' Sean asked.

'It's a wee area,' she said. 'Very tight an' cramped. Where we want, our target, the band assembly area where the parade takes place, there's an old people's home, a hostel used by walkers and even a school. There's a bank, always busy, an' a theatre, but it's the others I'm especially concerned about. I'm not sure we should be bombin' old people, backpackers an' children just to make a point. Particularly since few of 'em can be considered legitimate targets.'

'You're goin' soft,' Mad Dan said. 'You're a woman who's bombed a whole hotel, killin' people who just happened to be stayin' there, friend and foe alike. So what's the difference here?'

'That hotel was in Belfast. In a Loyalist area. It's fair to say that anyone stayin' there was doin' so in the full awareness of where they were stayin' and what it meant – loyalty to the Prods.'

'So?'

'So this isn't Northern Ireland. It isn't even related to it. The people livin' in that old people's home, the backpackers in the hostel and, more importantly, the wee children in that school aren't the same as the people who were stayin' in that hotel I bombed, not even remotely. They're innocent in the truest sense of the word and that makes me feel bad.'

'That's shite,' Mad Dan said brutally. 'There's no such thing as an innocent person when it comes to the struggle. Sure, innocent children have died in Belfast an' we don't like it but we've learnt to accept it. That's the cud we all chew over an' over. It's the vomit we swallow.'

'That doesn't make it right,' Mairead said. 'An' even if it did, those kids were in Belfast – our own – so at least, even if it wasn't admirable, it was our own we were makin' to pay the price. This is different. This isn't in the Province. An' we're not about to blow up just a few British soldiers – or even Irish children. That's what sticks in my craw.'

'She's right,' Sean said before Mad Dan could retort, which he was just about to do. Sean had read his guidebooks on the area and he, too, had his doubts. 'Most of the people on the Rock are of Italian, Portuguese and Spanish descent. Most are Roman Catholic. We could end up killin' a few Brit soldiers an' an awful lot of the others. I'm not sure if that'll do our cause any good. In fact it could set us back ten years. Mairead has a point here.'

'Shite!' Mad Dan exploded. 'The Rock of Gibraltar's another British Crown Colony – Christ, they've colonized everything – and that's the concept we're attackin', so let's go and do it.'

Taken aback that Mad Dan even knew a word like 'concept', Sean did not reply and instead distracted himself by gazing out of the window of the car. Having already passed through Torremolinos and Benalmádena-Costa, they were racing along the constantly curving racetrack of a highway towards Fuengirola.

'Still in Marbella?' Mad Dan asked.

'Aye,' Mairead replied. 'The other car's in the car park of my hotel and we'll talk to our demolitions man when we get there. He'll be expectin' us in the bar in an hour and so far we're on time.'

'He's Irish?'

'Ackaye.'

'Where does he get his groceries?'

'Brings it over from Morocco in a fancy boat owned by a wealthy English arms dealer. The boat's berthed in Puerto Banus and few questions are asked. The owner's been resident here for years and pisses money in all the right directions, so he has dispensations.'

'Him an' the Pope,' Mad Dan said. 'Sure, don't some have all the luck?'

'Anyway,' Mairead continued, not amused at all by Mad Dan, 'he has the stuff stacked up in his fancy apartment in Sotogrande – the last place the Spanish police would think of. So we just need a date an' time.'

'I thought we had that,' Sean said.

'We have the date – the eighth – but I still have my doubts about the target, so that has to be sorted out.'

'You better sort it out quick, girl,' Mad Dan said, 'or Tyrone'll be lookin' you up with his Black an' Decker. You told him we were going to do this job and that's what he's expectin' – not some shite about hittin' innocent women and children. Pat just wants results.'

Mairead sighed. 'Sure, I know that.'

She had just come off the bypass around Fuengirola and was racing past the Playa de Calahonda, around the high-rise apartment blocks towering over the promenades that ran parallel to the beaches and the sea in the afternoon's shimmering light.

'I've already booked you into the hotel,' Mairead told them. 'No problem at all. As I'm payin' the bill you're both booked in under my false passport and don't have to sign in. We'll just be there tonight. Tomorrow we'll book out of the hotel and visit the Rock. If we decide to do the job, we'll phone for the second car and let our driver bring in the bomb. The blocker, this car, will leave the parking space and let the driver in with the bomb. He'll then leave the car, following us back across the border. When we detonate the bomb, which we'll do from the Spanish side, we'll avoid Málaga entirely – they'll

141

be checkin' everyone at that airport – and instead drive all the way across country to Bilbao and take the boat from there to Southampton. With luck, we should make it.'

She felt more confident having said it, but then Mad Dan leant a little sideways, breathing into her ear, to tell her in his frightening way: 'You just said: "If we decide to do the job."'

'Aye, I . . .'

He stabbed at her shoulder with his index finger – once, twice, three times. 'Well, I'm tellin' you, girl, there's nothin' to decide. Tyrone wondered about you, he had his doubts there, an' he sent me along to make sure that there was no backin' out. We're goin' to do it, you hear me? Fuck the Spanish and the Portuguese. Fuck the pensioners an' the backpackers and the so-called innocent children. We're going to bomb the shite out of that little England on Gibraltar an' that's all there is to it. Now let's get to the hotel.'

Mad Dan had long been confident of his ability to frighten people and he therefore thought it natural that Mairead did not respond to his tirade but merely drove on in silence until they arrived at Marbella and the kind of hotel he would normally not even have considered entering. Once out of the car, however, and walking to the bar where they were to meet the demolitions man, she stopped, turned to face him, poked her finger repeatedly in his chest as he had done to her, and whispered, as if not wanting Sean to hear: 'There *are* things to decide and I'm the one to decide them. While we're here, while we're not packing guns, you'll take orders from me. We're carryin' no weapons, McCann. We won't be picked up for that. Without a gun in your hand you're not nearly as strong as I am and don't ever forget it. Sure, I'm in charge here, Mister. I decide what's right and wrong. An' if I decide that we're not bombin' the Rock, then we *don't* bomb the Rock.'

'For God's sakes, girl, I just . . .'

'If you don't like it, leave. Explain that to Pat Tyrone. Go back an' tell him that you let a woman defeat you and then wait for his thanks. Meanwhile, whether you like it or not, I'll do what I think's right. So are you in or out, Mister?'

Mad Dan quivered with rage, opened and closed his mouth, breathed deeply, then eventually managed to control himself and whispered: 'I'm in.'

'Sure, that's a grand thing to hear. Now be careful what you say in this bar when we talk about business. This man, though he's always helped us out, is still an unknown quantity. He makes his money here – not in Northern Ireland – and that makes him suspect. Do you understand?'

'Ackaye.'

'Let's get on, then.'

Mairead led Mad Dan and Sean into the bar, where they found a suntanned Irishman, Neil Dogherty, wearing a flowered Hawaiian-style shirt, white trousers and flip-flops, a Rolex on his wrist, with what looked like a double gin awash with ice cubes on the table in front of him. He had one of those ready-made smiles that only fools trust but few can resist.

'Have you come?' he said.

'Ackaye,' Mairead replied, then introduced Sean and Mad Dan by the names they had on their false passports.

'Nice to meet you,' Dogherty said.

'And you,' Sean replied.

'Grand,' Mad Dan said. 'Sure, you look like a very healthy Irishman with that tan an' all.'

'Nearly ten years here by now,' Dogherty explained when they were all seated around the table and had ordered their

143

drinks, including another double gin for himself. 'So the suntan comes for free. As for the clothes, sure you couldn't wear them in Ireland, but they're natural here.'

'Must've cost a bob or two.'

Mairead cast a quick, nervous glance at Mad Dan, which he failed to notice.

'Enough,' the man said.

'You make a good livin' here, then.'

'Aye, it's all right.'

'Sellin' groceries to your fellow-countrymen instead of makin' a contribution.'

Now the arms dealer was looking uncomfortable. 'Sure, a man has to eat,' he said.

'Aye, don't we all?' Mad Dan replied with a sneer.

'So,' Mairead broke in. 'Can we pick up the groceries?'

'They're all ready,' Dogherty said, referring to the Semtex and detonators paid for in advance when Dogherty had met her in the same bar three days earlier. 'Sure, I've done all the shoppin'. My car's parked beside your Renault down below in the car park, so we just have to go down an' collect them.'

'Sure, that's grand,' Mairead said. 'I hate shoppin' when I don't know the language. Makes me feel a quare fool.'

'Aye,' Dogherty said with a broad grin. 'I used to feel that way myself, but my Spanish is pickin' up.'

'Must be grand to speak a foreign language,' Sean said with no trace of irony.

'Sure, it helps,' Dogherty told him. 'When in Spain, do what the Spaniards do. That law applies to everywhere.'

'Exceptin' Ireland,' Sean told him. 'In Ireland, the Irish language is for the minority an' I think that's real criminal.'

'Sure, it is, when you think about it,' Dogherty said, 'but what can you do? The Brits robbed us of our language as well as our freedom and it's possible we'll never get it back. These are quare times indeed.'

'We'll get it back,' Mad Dan said. 'Sure, that's part of why we're here. We're not here just to get a suntan and wear fancy clothes. We're here to buy groceries that some countrymen would offer us for free because they know what we're plannin' to do will help set Ireland free.'

'Don't tell me what you're plannin',' Dogherty replied, his suntanned face flushed with anger. 'That's not part of the deal.'

'I wouldn't deal with the likes of you,' Mad Dan said, 'if I had my own way. I'd stay clear of the smell of you and your groceries. You can take that as written.'

Mairead glared at him. Apart from the possibility that he might blow this deal with his insults, you could never tell where a wall was bugged, when a man had been wired, and Mad Dan was blabbing too much for her liking.

'Sure, let's all relax,' she said.

'Sure, what else are we here for?' Mad Dan asked with a crooked, malicious grin.

'To have a holiday,' Mairead said. 'To get pissed and get a suntan. To eat all those groceries Neil brought and wash them down with cheap wine. Sure, isn't life in Spain grand? Isn't that right, Sean?'

'Ackaye, this is a grand place to be. Sure, it's summer already. That's why I come here – for the sun. For the cheap booze and food. I've always loved it in Spain.'

'Me, too,' Mairead said. 'And talkin' about the groceries,' she added. 'Was the money enough?'

'Right as rain. You can have the change later.'

'Well, let's go an' eat.'

They all finished their drinks, then followed Dogherty out of the bar and down into the hotel's dimly lit underground car park. There, as Dogherty had stated, they found his gleaming Audi 80 parked beside their rented white Renault 5. No further transactions were necessary and when the Semtex, already packed into a bomb made by Dogherty, was passed with the detonators from the boot of the Audi into the much smaller boot of the Renault, Dogherty placed his hand on Mairead's shoulder and said: 'Thanks for the business. Sure, come back anytime.'

Mairead did not smile. 'If this lot's not to standard,' she said, 'we'll come back to find you.'

The smile froze on Dogherty's face, became a grimace of fear, then returned to the semblance of good humour. 'Sure, you've no need to worry,' he said. 'Certain people I wouldn't cross.'

'Make sure you don't.'

Shaking his head from side to side, as if saying, 'What next?', Dogherty climbed into his car and roared off, leaving the other three standing beside the white Renault in the dimly lit, concrete wilderness of the car park. They all gazed down at the boot for some time, breathing heavily, saying nothing, as if hypnotized, or possibly frightened, by what was in there.

After a long silence Mairead took a deep breath and said: 'Right. So everything's set. Tomorrow we'll take the other car over to the Rock and check the target area again. If we decide to do it – if *I* decide we do it – we'll phone the driver, who's here in the hotel, and tell him to bring this car across. If we decide not to do it – if *I* decide that – then we'll come back here, get rid of this stuff, and head back to Málaga. Now let's get back to the hotel. Right?'

'Right,' Sean said.

There was a long, uncomfortable silence before Mad Dan, trying to control himself, nodded and said: 'Right.'

With everything arranged, they all went to their separate rooms and lay down in darkness. Mairead couldn't sleep at all, Sean had dreams of death and destruction, but Mad Dan slept the sleep of a child with his thumb in his mouth, at peace with the world.

The next morning, still undecided, they drove to Gibraltar.

12

Three days before the assumed date of the attack, shortly after the arrival of the three terrorists at Málaga had been reported to British Intelligence by Madrid's ever-alert Servicios de Información, the Special Projects Team, including the SAS, were flown into Gibraltar to await the arrival of the IRA bombers. The eleven members of the team, including the four-man SAS CQB team and two Special Branch women, arrived over a period of days and finally assembled at the Rock Hotel on Friday 5 March.

Gathering in other parts of the Rock was a swarm of security people of both sexes, mainly from MI5, augmented by local Special Branch personnel, to act as watchers and as an armed reserve.

That evening, in a room in the Rock Hotel, the SAS tactical leader, Captain Mike Edwards, introduced the two MI5 women who would work with the SAS men in tackling the terrorists when they arrived. Dressed in deliberately chosen plain clothes – blouse, skirt, short jackets and flat shoes, in keeping with local styles – both women, in their early twenties, were slim, attractive, good-humoured and surprisingly tough.

'These two ladies are from MI5,' Captain Edwards said to his gathered men, 'and have been assigned as plain-clothes watchers who'll follow both the terrorists and you lot while keeping in touch with operational control via Landmasters. This is Mary Hattersley,' he continued, indicating the smaller, blonde woman. He then pointed to the taller brunette and said: 'And this is Barbara Jennings. You may address them by their first names, just as you do each other.'

'How are you?' Sergeant Carruthers asked distractedly, keen to get on with the business in hand.

'Fine, thank you,' Mary Hattersley said.

'Welcome to the SAS,' Sergeant Ainsworth said.

'Thanks, Sarge,' Barbara Jennings said.

'Good to have you aboard,' Corporal Dymock said. 'You're a sight for sore eyes.'

'I'll second that,' Corporal Billings said.

'My two corporals aren't as rakish as they sound and look,' Captain Edwards said slyly. 'They're actually both engaged to be married to very nice girls.'

'Congratulations,' Mary Hattersley said.

'Gee, thanks, Captain,' Dymock practically whined.

'Shot down in my prime,' Billings added. 'It's great to be in the SAS.'

'All right, you two,' Carruthers reprimanded them, wanting to get on with the business at hand. 'Stop fooling around. OK, boss, the floor's all yours.'

As his four men, all wearing civilian clothes – casual jackets, open-necked shirts, jeans and trainers – broke into cheesy grins, Edwards introduced them to the ladies, pointing to each in turn as he called out their names. They're all brighter than they look,' he explained, 'though that may not be saying much.'

The two groups, men and women, smiled again at each other, then settled back to listen to the 'Head Shed'.

'These four men,' Captain Edwards began, addressing the ladies, 'will be split into two balanced CQB teams – by balanced, I mean one sergeant and one corporal in each team – and each of you ladies will follow one of those teams until the mission's been completed.'

'Are any other SAS men involved?' Barbara Jennings asked.

'Yes. We *do* have other SAS men on the Rock, but they'll be deployed at various points along the crossing from Spain right into Gibraltar.'

'Just who are we looking for?' Carruthers asked.

'You'll be informed in greater detail at the briefing scheduled to take place at midnight tonight. For now, I can only tell you that we're dealing with an IRA Active Service Unit that's planning to detonate a bomb here on the Rock. The purpose of the mission is to arrest them – arrest, disarm, and defuse the bomb. The people involved are all highly trained activists with considerable knowledge of both the making and use of bombs. They've also been known to have used a wide variety of personal weapons in the past and are knowledgeable about surveillance and interrogation techniques. In short, they're not back-street thugs, but highly trained, dangerous terrorists.'

'Are they under surveillance right now?' Ainsworth asked.

'Yes and no. The two men were observed arriving today by separate flights at Málaga, where they were met by a female and driven off by her in a rented white Renault 5. They're now somewhere between Málaga and the Rock.'

'You mean the Spanish police lost them,' the sergeant said contemptuously.

'Not that easy, I suspect,' Edwards replied generously, 'to keep your eye on three people driving a common type of car along the busy N340. Nevertheless, as they haven't yet shown up at the border, they're fully expected to materialize some time tomorrow, when they'll be allowed in.'

'Why not stop them there and then?'

'We have to ensure that no military action takes place on Spanish soil.'

'I'm glad to hear we're taking care not to embarrass the Spaniards,' Dymock said. 'Let's not spoil the tourist trade, eh?'

'So what are they actually here for?' Billings asked more seriously.

'The present action,' Edwards told him, 'is based on surveillance conducted on the same three when they came to Spain and Gibraltar previously – two in November, one earlier this month. For this reason we believe that they've returned to plant a bomb at the location of the Changing of the Guard and band parade ceremony, now set for 8 March, in three days' time. We also have reason to believe that they'll use a large bomb designed to kill as many soldiers as possible, as well as the civilians watching the event. That bomb will probably be detonated by remote control, almost certainly with a button control carried by at least one, and possibly all three, of the terrorists.'

'Which means that if confronted, the terrorists might instantly detonate the bomb,' Carruthers said.

'Correct. We also believe that these three extremely dangerous individuals will be armed and, if challenged, won't think twice about using their weapons.'

'So though the intention is to arrest and disarm them, and defuse the bomb, we have to bear in mind that if given enough time they'll use their weapons and probably press the button too.'

'Correct.'

'That doesn't give us any time at all to decide what to do – either shout a warning and arrest, or shoot to kill.'

Edwards sighed. 'I'm afraid not.'

'Do they plan to make the bomb here on the Rock or are they bringing it in?' asked Ainsworth.

'Based on information received from MI5, we believe that they'll arrive here by car and that the car will contain a bomb and won't be just a blocker.'

'I'm sorry,' Mary Hattersley interjected, 'but I'm not familiar with that terminology. What's a "blocker"?'

'An empty vehicle used to occupy a space that will subsequently be filled by the car containing the bomb. Usually the blocker will be driven into the nearest convenient parking space a few days before the day chosen for the bombing. Should any search be made of the cars parked in that area, the blocker will be found to be safe. Then, on the day set for the actual bombing, sometimes mere minutes before the time chosen for detonation, the blocker will be driven away and its space immediately taken up with the car containing the bomb. The driver then leaves the second car, gets well clear of the area and finally either he or another member of the ASU team detonates the bomb by remote control. That's what we believe is going to happen in this particular instance.'

'At what point do we use our weapons?' Carruthers asked.

'I repeat: the purpose of the mission is arrest, disarm and defuse the bomb. However, weapons may be used should you – and I quote from the official directive – "have reasonable grounds for believing that an act is being committed which would endanger life or lives and if there is no other way of preventing that other than with firearms". Read that as you may.'

'So if we have to shoot, we shoot to kill?' Carruthers asked.

'You neutralize, yes. These people may have a button control or hidden weapons, so you shoot and keep shooting until their hands are well away from the body.' Though the men were grinning, the women glanced uneasily at each other as Edwards studied his watch. 'It's nearly midnight,' he said. 'Time for the official briefing. Follow me, please.'

After leading them out of the room and down the stairs to the hotel car park, Edwards personally drove them in a borrowed Ford Cortina along the dark, lamplit Europa Road to the Lathbury Barracks. When they had each shown their personal identification card to the armed guard at the steel gates they were allowed to drive through to a car park filled with British Army troop lorries, jeeps, some Saracen armoured cars, a few ambulances and unmarked 'Q' cars. They clambered out of the car, which Edwards carefully locked, and marched to the solid steel door of a lift that carried them up to an ultra-secure briefing centre hidden deep within the gun galleries of the Rock itself. As Edwards knew from personal experience, these secret galleries and caverns also contained a model of a 'typical Ulster village' where soldiers, including the SAS, were trained in counter-insurgency techniques. He did not, however, impart this knowledge when he left the lift and led his six-strong team into a large hall where other elements of the Flavius force, about fifty people in all, including carefully screened members of the local police, were waiting for the briefing to commence.

Seated at the long table on the raised dais overlooking the men and women in rows of steel-framed chairs was the advisory group in charge of the briefing. Studying them, Edwards recognized some British Intelligence officers from MI5 and MI6, the chief of Gibraltar's Special Branch, the Deputy Commissioner of Gibraltar, and two Lieutenant

Colonels, one from HQ Special Forces, the other from 22 SAS. This, Edwards knew, was also the team that would advise the Police Commissioner, who was nominally in charge of law enforcement.

The briefing opened with the head of Special Branch repeating the official objectives of Operation Flavius and the 'rules of engagement', including the need for 'minimum' force, which contradicted what Edwards had just told his men in private. 'In other words,' he summarized, after droning on for ten minutes to the increasingly bored, sometimes confused SAS men, 'every effort should be made to protect life, to foil the bomb attempt, to make arrests and to take custody of the prisoners. Any questions?'

'Yes, sir,' Edwards responded promptly. 'Do you now know the identities of the terrorists?'

'Yes. Daniel McCann, Sean Savage and Mairead Farrell.'

'A psychopath and a female fanatic,' Carruthers whispered to his fellow-sergeant, Ainsworth, 'with an unknown quantity in between. It doesn't look good to me, mate.'

'The three terrorists,' the head of Special Branch continued, as if to confirm what Carruthers had whispered, 'are believed to be armed and highly dangerous – so dangerous, in fact, that we can't leave this job to the local police. That's why the SAS were called in. Though the Spanish police lost track of the terrorists soon after they left Málaga, they're believed to be heading for Gibraltar in a rented white Renault 5 containing a bomb. But at this point we don't know exactly where they are. And nor do we know exactly when they plan to cross into Gibraltar.'

'There are no Spanish representatives at this briefing?' Edwards asked in disbelief.

'No.'

'So we can't ask what the Spanish authorities are doing about a large bomb being driven around one of the most densely populated tourist areas in Spain.'

'No.'

'Do the Gibraltar police know that a high-powered anti-terrorist operation is going on under their very noses?'

'Some are uninformed,' the head of Special Branch replied with a steely smile. 'Others have been deliberately misinformed for security reasons.'

'So can we take it,' the British Army Lieutenant Colonel asked, 'that the Spanish authorities – and therefore, by implication, the British authorities – may indeed have the terrorists under surveillance, but actually *want* them to enter Gibraltar in order that they can be either arrested or neutralized?'

'You may deduce from it what you like, but I simply cannot answer that question.'

'How will the terrorists be dealt with?' the Police Commissioner asked, looking worried.

The head of Special Branch nodded at the SAS Lieutenant Colonel sitting to his left, indicating that he should answer the question. 'A four-man team wearing civilian clothing and carrying radios and nine-millies – 9mm Browning High Power handguns,' the Lieutenant Colonel said, clarifying the term for those not familiar with SAS slang, 'will arrest the terrorists and allow the bomb to be defused. The other SAS men, supported by male and female watchers from MI5 and Special Branch, will be in various strategic positions from where they can track the terrorists' movements and, if necessary, lend support in a fire-fight. All will be in radio contact with an operations centre located here and commanded by Captain Edwards.'

'What about the legalities of this affair with particular regard to the laws of Gibraltar?' the Commissioner asked.

'A local policeman will be with the soldiers to act as witness and take any arrested terrorists into custody.'

'Are there any clearly defined rules for a situation such as this?' the Commissioner persisted. 'I mean in a situation where the attempted arrest could lead to a fire-fight or, even worse, to the setting off of the bomb by a button control?'

'The SOP – standard operating procedure – has been well rehearsed. Once the SAS men decide to make the arrest, they'll shout: "Stop! Police! Hands up!" If the terrorists comply, they'll be made to lie face down on the ground with arms away from the body, to ensure that they can't press the button or reach for their weapons. Should they attempt to do either before obeying the commands, the SAS will open fire. Any more questions?'

There were no more questions.

Back in the Rock Hotel in the early hours of Saturday 6 March, when the four men chosen for the assault team had gathered together for a 'Chinese parliament' – an informal discussion of tactics – with Captain Edwards, Sergeant Carruthers said bluntly: 'Now that the political and diplomatic bullshit is over, Captain, what's the real story regarding how we should tackle these murdering Paddies?'

'You heard the real story at the briefing,' Edwards replied disingenuously. 'And I'm sure you heard correctly.'

'But before the briefing, you said . . .'

'What I said was off the record, Sergeant.'

'A lot of what was said at that briefing was just rubbish kit,' Carruthers persisted. 'More dangerous to us than to the enemy. Never mind bloody minimum force! I want to know what we *really* do when push comes to shove.'

'Yes, sir, what *is* minimum force,' Dymock asked, 'in a situation like this?'

'Let's call it *reasonable* force,' Edwards told him. 'Shooting only if absolutely necessary and no more than's required.'

'That tells us a lot, boss,' Ainsworth said. 'What's reasonable in Northern Ireland might not be reasonable here. You've already said that if we shoot, we shoot to kill. Given what we've just heard about minimum force, can we take that as read?'

Well aware of the fact that if anything went wrong he would carry the can, Edwards replied carefully: 'I believe the orders provide for the use of lethal force for the preservation of life. In other words, if you think they're going to fire or press the button, you shoot before they can do so.'

'Do we have any proof that they'll be armed as the head of Special Branch said?' asked Carruthers.

'No, Sergeant, in truth we haven't. Given their track records, we can't imagine them coming here *unarmed* – but we don't have the proof.'

'So we stand the chance of shooting unarmed people.'

'Possibly unarmed – but almost certainly carrying a button-job. I think that's the clincher.'

'So if they offer any kind of resistance,' Dymock said, 'or even refuse to put up their hands, we don't hesitate to open fire.'

'No, you don't,' Edwards said.

'In that case, how many rounds?' Carruthers asked.

'You keep firing until the terrorist is no longer a threat.'

'If we do that, we could be accused of overkill.'

'A wounded terrorist – even mortally wounded – can still initiate the button to detonate a bomb. You must ensure that he or she doesn't get the chance to do so.'

'So even if he or she is down, we keep firing until we're absolutely sure that they've been neutralized.'

'Correct.'

'We'll only have the nine-milly?'

'Yes, only one handgun each. Each with four magazines – forty-eight shots per man. A total of 192 rounds between the four of you. The ammo, however, will be a new 9mm mix of British and French smokeless propellant. It emits less smoke and flash than traditional gunpowder.'

'And those two sexy ladies,' Dymock said. 'The MI5 watchers. What will they be doing while we're closing in on the terrorists?'

'They'll be giving us hand-jobs,' Billings said hopefully.

'To relieve the tension,' Dymock clarified.

'You two have filthy mouths,' Ainsworth said, 'and you're not concentrating, so shut up, listen and concentrate.'

'You men won't be able to take your eyes off the terrorists for a second,' Edwards explained. 'You'll have your nine-millies holstered in the cross-draw position under your jackets and you'll have to be ready to use them on the instant. This means, in effect, that you could find yourselves in a situation where you don't have time to communicate with me, even using the miniature microphones and ear-worn receivers. Those two sexy ladies, therefore – incidentally both well trained and highly efficient – will always be a short distance behind you and the terrorists, out of sight but in constant contact with the operational room, to call in a Quick Reaction Force if necessary. If, on the other hand, the QRF isn't required, but the terrorists have been neutralized, the watchers will call for a couple of Q cars to lift you out of the killing grounds before you're identified.'

'Well, *that's* a relief,' Ainsworth said.

'So what happens now?' Dymock asked, checking his watch and noting that it was nearly two in the morning of Sunday 6 March.

'Now you sleep,' Edwards told him, 'and hopefully wake refreshed tomorrow, prepared for anything.'

The Chinese parliament broke up and the CQB team retired to their beds in a British Army barracks not much different from the 'spider' back in Hereford. Given the dangerous task they had been set, they all slept surprisingly well.

13

Jolted out of their sleep by early alarm calls, the four SAS men rolled out of their beds in the Rock Hotel, showered, shaved and dressed in their civilian operational clothes, then went down to the dining-room for breakfast like normal residents, all sitting at separate tables and pretending not to know one another.

As they finished eating they left the restaurant one by one and made their way along Europa Road to the Lathbury Barracks, where, after showing their identification cards, they were admitted through the guarded steel gates. Each of them then walked to the steel lift that took them up into the network of gun galleries and caverns where the briefing centre was hidden, along with various military command centres and the mock Ulster village used for training purposes. There, in a small room containing only a rectangular wooden table with bench-style seats around the four walls, the men gathered together with Captain Edwards and the two MI5 watchers, the small, blonde-haired Mary Hattersley and the taller brunette, Barbara Jennings. Both women were dressed, as the day before, in relatively plain blouse, skirt, short jacket and flat shoes. Only Captain Edwards was in uniform, the

161

maroon beret with its winged-dagger SAS badge perched at a rakish angle on his head.

Behind Edwards was a cork pinboard covered with maps of the Rock of Gibraltar and photos of the three terrorists expected that day.

Four 9mm Browning High Power handguns were laid out on the table, each with a single fourteen-round magazine beside it and a leather holster with belt. At one end of the table there were two Pace Communications Ltd Landmaster III transceivers and four sets of Davies M135b covert microphones with accompanying ear-worn receivers, matching pairs of miniature radios and wrist-worn on-off switches.

'Morning, ladies and gentlemen,' Edwards said in his urbane manner. 'I trust you're all feeling bright and chirpy after a good night's sleep.' When this greeting was returned with various murmured salutations, Edwards picked up a pointer and tapped it against the photos of the three terrorists, one after the other: 'Sean Savage,' he said, tapping the head-shot of the younger man. 'Mad Dan McCann,' he said, tapping the nose of the older man. 'And this,' he continued, tapping the image of a strikingly attractive woman, 'is Mairead Farrell.'

Lowering the pointer and looking at everyone in turn, Edwards saw that even the younger men, Dymock and Billings, were listening intently and not casting flirtatious glances at Mary Hattersley and Barbara Jennings. Pleased, he raised the pointer to the board and again tapped each of the three photos.

'Study these faces well. Let them burn into your memory. Make sure that when you go out into the streets of Gibraltar, you don't mistake anyone else for these people.' Tapping the photos of the two men in turn, he said: 'These are the two who turned up in Málaga last November and paid a couple of visits to the Rock. The woman arrived a week ago, visited the Rock just about every day, and was observed yesterday afternoon greeting Savage and McCann when they arrived for the second time at Málaga airport. We still don't know where they are at this moment, but we're expecting them to turn up here sometime today. If this is the case, we must assume that they're here to do serious damage.'

'So this is the day we stop them,' Ainsworth said.

'Correct. For this purpose you four men will be divided into two-man teams. Team One will be Sergeant Carruthers and Corporal Dymock, Team Two Sergeant Ainsworth and Corporal Billings. You four have been picked because it was considered wise for each team to have a lead and a backup man – a sergeant and a corporal – and, in particular, because you're all proven experts at the double tap. And this is a CQB double-tap operation.'

'You hear that, ladies?' Dymock said with a cocky grin. 'We're the best of the best.'

'We're so thrilled just to be here,' Barbara Jennings said deadpan. 'It's an honour, believe me.'

'We believe you,' Billings said, grinning.

'Modesty becomes you,' Carruthers told the corporals. 'Now shut up and listen to the boss. This is no time for silly games.'

But he wasn't angry. He was experienced enough to know that the younger men had decided to flirt with the women in order to settle their own nerves. This was a dangerous, unpredictable operation and all of them knew it.

'Don't forget,' Edwards said, 'when you're out in the street that you'll have backup not only from these two fine ladies here, but also from armed Gibraltar policemen, other MI5 surveillance officers, and the rest of the SAS men flown in yesterday. Though keeping out of sight, they'll have you under

163

surveillance at all times and be ready to make an urgent appearance should it be necessary.'

'When does all this start?' Ainsworth asked.

'A local Special Branch officer is working hand in glove with Spanish security on the Spanish side of the border. He's aware, as are the Spanish, that we're expecting the three terrorists today – he knows there are two men and a woman – and that they're travelling in a hired white Renault 5. He also has the registration number, which was picked up from the Avis office in Málaga. Whether the terrorists arrive together or separately, the Special Branch officer will be able to identify them and will notify my command centre of their arrival. When he does, you'll move out and track them down, following directions transmitted to your covert receivers. When you see the terrorists, you'll attempt to get into a position where you can challenge them, giving them the chance to surrender. From that point on you must use your own initiative, bearing in mind what was said formally at the briefing and what I personally told you rather more informally.'

'That's walking a tightrope,' Carruthers said.

'I know, Sarge, and I don't like it either, but we'll have to live with it. Are there any last questions?'

All the men shook their heads.

'Good. Your weapons are on the table.' Edwards jabbed his index finger at the four handguns spread out neatly on the table. 'One nine-milly and one magazine each. That's it. That's all you get.'

As the men were loading the magazines, which made a sharp, metallic sound as they were slotted in, Edwards turned to Mary Hattersley and Barbara Jennings. 'You ladies,' he said, 'will be equipped with one Landmaster III transceiver each, tuned to this operational HQ, where I'll be in charge.

Your brief is to stay well behind the CQB teams following the terrorists and to keep me informed of what's happening. Most importantly, as stated yesterday, once the terrorists are apprehended, you'll call in the transport to take them away and also the bomb-disposal team who're on stand-by here. Finally, should the CQB teams be forced to neutralize the terrorists, you'll immediately call up two Q cars to remove them before they're identified. Any questions?'

Mary Hattersley shook her head from side to side.

'No,' Barbara Jennings said.

'Good. Now pick up your transceivers and keep them with you at all times – at least from now until the mission has been completed and my men are out of town.'

As the two MI5 watchers picked up and checked their transceivers, Edwards turned back to his men and checked that they were all wearing their Brownings in the proper cross-draw position up under their jackets, around the back where they could be easily withdrawn. Satisfied, he nodded towards the miniature communications equipment still left on the table. 'One set to each man,' he said. 'Please put them on and check that they're working. They should already be tuned in to the command centre, and someone at the other end, in my HQ, is waiting to hear if they're working. Just state your rank and name. When the man on the other end of the line responds, say: "Over and out." Now get to it, chaps.'

Already familiar with this kind of communications equipment, which they had used in the OP in Belfast when spying on Mairead Farrell and the others entering and leaving the Republican pub across the road, the men had no trouble in sorting out the various components: M135b covert microphone attached to a standard safety-pin; miniature microphones positioned in the collar of the shirt; the on-off switch taped to the wrist of the hand not used for firing the handgun; and two miniature radios hidden on the person; one tuned into the military command network, there deep within the Rock, the other to the surveillance network, including the Landmark III transceivers in the care of Mary Hattersley and Barbara Jennings.

When everything was in place, the men took turns to identify themselves through the microphones, checking that they could indeed be heard where they were supposed to be tuned to. With everything deemed to be in working order, they turned back to Edwards.

'What now?' Carruthers asked.

'Now we wait,' Edwards told him.

The local Special Branch officer, Detective Constable Wilby, on duty on the Spanish side of the border, was seated in an enclosed room beside a Spanish immigration officer, Juan Ribera. Both men were facing a screen on to which the Spaniards were projecting images of passport photographs and numbers taken from people crossing the border by foot. Also, car registration numbers were being passed to Wilby by Ribera, who was in contact by telephone with his Spanish colleagues watching the cars go through.

Aware of the fact that the white Renault 5 hired by the terrorists at Málaga airport might have been changed for another car by now, Wilby was checking the registration numbers given to him by Ribera against a list of all the available rental cars along the coast between Málaga and Algeciras – enough to give him a headache. He was also checking them against a second list of suspect registration numbers, taken from Spanish and Gilbraltarian police files of cars either stolen or known to have been used for illegal purposes.

Wilby had been instructed to look out for two men and a woman named as Savage, McCann and Farrell, but travelling under false passports, the details of which had been given to him by his superiors. Pinned to the wall in front of him, just below the window, were photographs of the three wanted persons. Wilby was in contact by personal radio with Captain Edwards in his HQ in the command centre and prepared to call him the minute the white Renault 5 or the terrorists on foot were sighted outside. He was also passing on details of passports and car registration numbers given to him by the Spaniards, where he thought they had, or may have, relevance.

He had been doing this all morning and was becoming monumentally bored, convinced that it was all a hoax, when, just before 12.30 p.m., Ribera listened to the telephone, scribbling down a number as he did so, then tore the paper out of the notebook and handed it to him.

It was a Spanish registration number.

'A white Renault 5,' Ribera told him. 'Just coming through.'

When Wilby saw the car, with an Avis sticker on it, approaching from the gates of passport control and customs, he became very excited and checked the registration number against the one he had listed for the terrorists' rented vehicle. It was the same number.

He watched as the white Renault 5 drove past him and across the runway towards Winston Churchill Avenue, which led to the central shopping area of Gibraltar, including the band assembly area. There was only one person in the vehicle: a male driver.

As instructed, Wilby did nothing to stop the car. He did, however, hurriedly telephone Captain Edwards at the operations centre.

'Mike?'

'Yes.'

'Our white Renault has just gone through and is heading for the centre of town, probably for the car park.'

'Were all three subjects in it?'

'No, only the driver – a male.'

'Right. The other two are either coming in a second car or have been dropped off on the Spanish side and will cross by foot. If they're in a car, they might be difficult to spot, but please do your best.'

Two hours later, Wilby saw two faintly familiar faces – one male and one female – emerging from the sea of people crossing by foot into Gibraltar. When he glanced down at the photos pinned to the wall beneath the window, he was able instantly to match their faces with those of Daniel McCann and Mairead Farrell. The woman he would have recognized a mile away from her pale face framed by long, dark hair.

Now even more excited, Wilby watched the man and woman as they passed his hidden room and walked on towards the runway that led to the Rock. He then picked up the telephone and dialled the command centre again.

'Mike! McCann and Farrell have just passed through on foot and are walking towards the airstrip right now.'

'Good work,' Edwards replied. 'That's all three of them in. Thanks a million, Ken.'

'My pleasure,' Wilby said.

Dropping the telephone, Wilby continued to watch the couple as they crossed the runway and eventually were lost to sight somewhere in the heat haze along Winston Churchill Avenue. Even when they were out of sight, he kept looking towards the Rock, expecting to hear or see something dramatic at any moment.

In fact, forty-five minutes passed before the phone rang again. When Wilby picked it up, noting that it was exactly a quarter past three, he was informed that the IRA team had been spotted on the Rock and that he could now leave and return to his own HQ there.

Delighted that things had gone so smoothly, Wilby left the concealed office, climbed on to his motor-bike and raced across the airstrip, along Winston Churchill Avenue, then into Smith Darrien Road. Bogged down in traffic in the latter thoroughfare, he slowed practically to a crawl, then had to stop altogether.

There, mere yards away, he saw Mad Dan McCann and Mairead Farrell, walking side by side and, as he watched, exchanging newspapers. Sean Savage was trailing close behind them.

Mesmerized by the sight of all three terrorists so close to him, the Special Branch man had no way of knowing that all three of them would be dead within minutes.

14

Mairead Farrell was dressed in a skirt and blouse, Daniel McCann was in grey trousers and a white shirt, and Sean Savage was wearing grey trousers and a sober pinstripe jacket when they descended to the basement car park of their hotel in Marbella. First they checked that the Semtex and the detonators in one of the white Renaults were still in good shape, then they climbed into the other Renault, and Sean drove them out of the garage, leaving the car containing the bomb still in its parking space.

'I still don't think this is right,' Mad Dan said as Sean joined the N340 in the direction of Gibraltar. 'We shouldn't leave that bomb-car so long in the car park. Sure, we should get it over an' done with. Set the bomb off today.'

'I don't give a damn what you think,' Mairead replied. 'I still have my doubts about this job and I want 'em resolved. So we'll drive to Gibraltar and look around one last time, then decide yes or no. If yes, we'll do the job two days from now, right in the middle of the Changin' of the Guard. You want somethin' outrageous, Dan? Then that should do the trick. Not today, not tomorrow, but the next day, when the place'll be packed with bystanders. Isn't that what you want?'

'Sure, I'm not convinced we should do it at all,' Sean told her, 'but if we do, then we should do it on Tuesday. I agree on that much.'

Sean was still feeling haunted after a night of vivid nightmares in which he'd seen the ghosts of all the dead of all the buildings he had bombed in the past: bloody, broken, scorched, stripped to the bone, howling out in a manner so dreadful that it went beyond agony. Sean was torn by what he did, which is why he was quiet about it. On the one hand he believed that a man should fight for his beliefs; on the other he had never bombed an inhabited building without suffering the torments of the damned.

Essentially religious, steeped in history and the beauty of the Irish language, Sean lived as intimately with guilt as a man could do without being destroyed by it. His silence was based on shame. He had tried to bury it, but failed. In the incandescence of his dreams he saw hell's fires waiting to claim him. He believed in his country, was willing to fight for it, but increasingly he bore the burden of guilt over those he had killed. So he had doubts about Gibraltar and was glad he was not alone.

'We should at least be armed when we go there,' Mad Dan insisted, growing ever more frustrated but still shocked by the ruthlessness shown so clearly by Mairead the previous day. 'Sure, bejasus, that place is filled with Brit soldiers and we might have to . . .'

'I've told you before and I'm telling you again,' Mairead said, glancing back over her shoulder to where Mad Dan was sitting in the rear seat. 'We're taking no guns. Those things invite trouble. There could be X-ray machines at those border posts and if there are we'd be licked before we started. So no guns, an' that's final. No guns and no bombs today.'

And maybe not even on Tuesday, she thought. Not while Mad Dan is with us.

She felt exhausted and nervous from lack of sleep, not having slept a wink the previous night. She'd tossed and turned, recalling the Conway Hotel all of ten years ago, the smoke and the fire and the ruins, with the dead and injured buried under rubble, the latter screaming for help. In order to carry out that bombing Mairead had been compelled to bury a small, secret part of herself. But once the deed had been accomplished and she'd found herself in prison, her moments of guilt and horror, which came fleetingly but often, had gradually faded away as she prided herself on the admiration of her fellow prisoners.

'Sure, you sacrificed yourself for your country,' they constantly told her. 'You're the best of the best, girl.'

Such praise had sustained her for the first few of her ten long years, but eventually, as her first prison friends were released, she had withdrawn into herself. Eventually, as she felt herself ageing within those walls, gradually being drained dry, she had succumbed to relentless insomnia and started taking sedation to help her sleep. By the time she got out of prison, ten years older, she was a shadow of the woman she had been, albeit still beautiful.

It was her beauty that had saved her, bringing Tom Riley to her. God, yes, even now when she thought of Tom, she swelled with pride and pain. She had met him in that pub, the one she was in when he died, and the meeting of their minds, their mutual commitment to the cause, had soon led to physical affirmation and the flowering of true love. Then Tom had blown himself up and after that it had *all* blown apart: all her great hopes for the future.

Had it not been for the Prods, Tom wouldn't have died. Mairead blamed them even for that. Yes, she hated the Prods.

173

But did she? Not really. It was the Brits she hated, for setting the Prods against the Catholics and creating a war. She knew that right enough, lived by it, killed for it; but she had always tried to remember that there were limits and that one had to abide by them. The Rock of Gibraltar could represent one of those limits and she was trying to work it out.

A bomb outrage was one thing – nasty but necessary. But the Rock of Gibraltar was a British Crown Colony – not really British; just another colonized piece of land, ruthlessly stolen, like Northern Ireland – and as Sean had rightly said, it was filled with foreigners, including old people and children, who in no way represented Britain or even supported it. To bomb such a place, particularly where they were planning to do so – a school, a Jewish old people's home, a walkers' hostel, never mind the foreign tourists – might be something more than a bloody outrage; it would be downright wicked.

God might never forgive her.

'I feel naked going into a British Crown Colony without a gun in my belt,' Mad Dan said, glancing out of the rear window of the car as Sean turned off the N340 and headed for the border at La Línea. 'Sure, I might as well have no pants on.'

'Sure, that's a sight I'd rather not see,' Mairead said caustically, not caring if she angered him, thinking: God, no wonder I have doubts! With a vampire like this by your side, you're bound to start worrying. Him and his guns and all . . .

'Sure, I'm choosy about who I drop 'em for,' Mad Dan sneered, 'and yer not on my list.'

'Thank God for that.'

Mad Dan quivered with rage and had to fight to control himself. He was under strict instructions from Pat Tyrone to take his orders from this woman, but even though she'd bombed a Prod hotel ten years ago, he couldn't stand the sight of her. Proud in her beauty. Too proud for the likes of him. Brushing back her hair from her eyes and looking down her nose at him. Mad Dan wanted to crush her. He wanted to be in charge. That Rock was a fucking British colony and he wanted to bomb the place. Take all the bastards out. Shock the whole bloody world. Pay the British government back for the eight good men killed by the SAS at Loughgall and show them that they could never feel safe any more – anywhere.

But were they going to do it? No, they were just looking. They were going like bloody tourists to see the sights and twiddle their thumbs. This damned woman was indecisive. Sean wasn't much better. Here he was with a woman who'd bombed a hotel ten years ago – done nothing since, mind – and a kid who cycled about the countryside and studied history and Gaelic. What a pair to be stuck with! Both whimpering about what was right. Well, by God, *he'd* show 'em what was right if he got half the chance.

Mad Dan was simmering silently, boiling up inside. He'd come here to do some serious damage and this bitch could well put a stop to it. Besides which, she practically sneered at him every time she opened her mouth.

Just give me a Webley pistol, he thought, and she'll be the first to go. Never mind the fuckin' Brits.

But he didn't have a Webley – he had nothing – so he just sat there simmering . . .

As the car drove into the ugly, ramshackle border town of La Línea, Mairead said to Sean: 'Try to find a bar or café near the border, where you can leave me and Dan to warm our bums for a couple of hours while you go on ahead in the car and find a good parkin' space.'

'Sure, why are we doin' that?' Mad Dan asked. 'We don't have any weapons or bombs, so why can't we all drive on, like?'

'I know we've had no trouble with the authorities so far – not when you two came last November; nor this trip with the three of us – but there's a quare chance the bastards are watchin' us an' bidin' their time. Sure, if Sean's seen drivin' in alone an' parkin' the car – an' if it's true, as some suspect, that he's under Brit surveillance – then the police here just might check his car – and if they do, they'll find nothin'. Then, if we decide to do it, we can drive in two days later an' replace his car with the bomb-car. Can yer thick head digest that?'

'Ackaye, it can,' Mad Dan said, choking back his rage. ''Cause it isn't that thick, girl.'

'Sure, we don't need to argue among ourselves,' Sean reprimanded them with surprising firmness. 'What Mairead says makes sense to me, Dan. She's simply suggestin' that we use this car as a blocker and I fully agree.'

'Aye, right,' Mad Dan replied, almost bursting with the desire to look down the sight of a Webley at Mairead Farrell's haughty head. 'Anything you say, like.'

'Good,' Mairead said.

Sean drew up outside a café near the La Línea gate. It was nearly 12.30 and the sun was high in the sky, making those in the car, all used to the cold of Belfast, feel hot and sweaty.

'This'll do,' Mairead said, opening the door and slipping out of the car as Mad Dan reluctantly did the same behind her. Walking around the car, she bent down to Sean's open window and said: 'Just drive on through, park as close as you can get to the band assembly area – there's a car park almost facin' it – and then go for a bit of a gander. At half past two, we'll walk across and meet you in the car park. That's exactly two hours from now. That's a reasonable enough time to discourage any connection between us if we're all bein' watched. All right?'

'Ackaye,' Sean said.

When Sean drove off, passing unchecked through the La Línea gate, Mairead and Mad Dan took a table outside the Spanish bar – it was already warm enough for that – and ordered a couple of beers, which would last them longer than coffee.

When the white Renault disappeared from view, obviously crossing the runway on its way to the centre of Gibraltar, Mairead pulled a romantic novel out of her handbag and started reading.

Mad Dan, who knew she didn't want to talk to him, simply sighed, inhaled on a cigarette and blew smoke rings.

Two hours and three beers later, at precisely 2.30, Mairead and Mad Dan entered Gibraltar on foot and met up with Sean by the car.

Even as the three terrorists were getting together, they were being observed from a short distance by the two MI5 women. When she saw the meeting being completed, Mary Hattersley gave an imperceptible hand signal to Barbara Jennings, indicating that she should do nothing, then raised her transceiver to her lips and spoke quietly into it, telling Captain Edwards, in his HQ in the command centre, that the three targets had finally met up and were standing by their hired car.

'Let's go, men!' Sergeant Carruthers snapped urgently at a signal from Edwards.

The four SAS men, still wearing civilian clothes, hurried out of the building.

15

Crossing into Gibraltar at 12.30 in the white Renault 5 after dropping off Mairead and Mad Dan, Sean was impressed by the sheer size of the Rock, which appeared to rise towards the azure sky and grow bigger as he moved closer to it. Having familiarized himself with its history, he knew that it consisted mainly of limestone and had many caves and tunnels that had been excavated for defensive purposes and were still being used by the Brits and the Gibraltarian police. Gibraltar, though steeped in both real history and mythology – it was supposed to be one of the Pillars of Hercules, after all – was now a fortified naval base and much of the town, which had been partly built on land reclaimed from the surrounding sea, was occupied by army barracks, naval establishments and hospitals. As such, no matter how romantic it seemed to Sean, it made a legitimate target.

After driving through the winding, packed streets of the central shopping area, he eventually passed between the Hambros Bank and the band assembly area. Following the road around, he passed the Jewish Old People's Home, then the Toc-H Hostel and the Bishop Fitzgerald School by the High Stone Wall. Just past the school was the entrance to the car park. Sean collected his ticket as he drove in, then parked the car.

By this time, equipped with their concealed transceivers broadcasting on a network dedicated to the operation. Mary Hattersley and Barbara Jennings were making their way down into the centre of town to locate the white Renault 5 and, with luck, its driver. Just as they were approaching Main Street, Sean was leaving the car park to wander around and have a bit of a 'gander' that might help with decisions regarding the placing of the bomb two days from now, during the band parade ceremony.

Knowing that the only place to park was the car park, Hattersley and Jennings, taking slightly different courses and a good distance apart, made their way there. While Hattersley waited outside to check the people swarming through the surrounding streets, Jennings entered and walked along the rows of cars until she saw the terrorists' car. Having confirmed that it had the same registration number as the one she had been given, she put out a general message – to Captain Edwards and to the four SAS men now hurrying down from the Lathbury Barracks – confirming that the car had been parked, but that the driver was nowhere in sight.

The four SAS men in civilian clothing immediately separated into two teams, each of which took a different direction into the centre of town.

While Jennings remained in the car park, keeping a discreet distance from the parked white Renault 5, Hattersley wandered up and down the High Stone Wall and Line Wall Road, looking for Sean Savage, whom she hoped to recognize from the photo she was carrying on her person. She had studied that picture many times and felt sure she would know him, but she still wanted the photo for confirmation. In the event, it was another hour before she finally spotted him.

Wearing a pinstripe jacket and grey slacks, he was standing beside a group of Japanese tourists close to the band assembly area, which he was carefully studying. Removing the photo from her pocket, Hattersley checked that it was indeed Savage. When she had confirmed, she notified the others on the transceiver.

'We're on our way,' Carruthers responded. 'Don't let him out of your sight. Over and out.'

Sean walked away from the band assembly area, trying to act like a normal tourist, and indeed feeling a certain regret that he could not take the cable car up the face of the mighty Rock and have a look, in particular, at the Barbary apes that roamed free up there. At the same time, Mairead looked at her watch, saw that it was just after 2p.m. and told Mad Dan that it was time for them to leave the bar and enter Gibraltar.

'About time,' Mad Dan growled.

Placing her book in her bag, Mairead pushed her chair back, then stood up and walked with Mad Dan to the La Línea gate. The officer at passport control barely glanced at their false passports, apparently noting only the fact that they were British. Within minutes they were walking across the runway and heading for town.

They were unaware of the fact that they had been identified by the staff of passport control and their presence in Gibraltar made known, by phone and radio, to Edwards, his four SAS men and the MI5 watchers.

It was exactly 2.30.

By this time, Sean had wandered back to the car park, as arranged, and was already waiting by the white Renault when the others showed up.

'Everything all right so far?' Mairead asked him.

'Ackaye. Sure, I'm just another tourist. There's so many people here, we'll just be tourists in the crowd. No problem at all.'

'Let's take another look,' Mairead said.

It was 2.50 when the three terrorists walked out of the car park and headed for the Alameda Gardens, a short distance away. They were being followed at a discreet distance by Hattersley and Jennings, who were transmitting a running commentary on the trio's movements to the two-man SAS teams.

As a result, the SAS teams were also tracking the three terrorists and waiting for an opportune moment to challenge them, preferably well away from the central shopping area, crowded mainly with tourists.

'Sure, this place is a piece of piss,' Mad Dan said as he and the others rested in the shade of the Alameda Gardens. 'As Sean said, there's so many people runnin' about we'll just be thought of as other bloody tourists.'

'It's busy enough, all right,' Mairead said. 'For such a small place, there's certainly a lot goin' on, like.'

'An' in two days' time,' Mad Dan reminded her, 'when the actual Changin' of the Guard's goin' on, there's goin' to be even more people. This place'll be like an anthill.'

Sean, still romantically inclined and recalling what he'd read about the place, pointed up the face of the mighty Rock, above the tiers of houses perched precariously above the old defensive walls, to where it became a series of sheer, inaccessible cliffs and sand slopes surmounted by sun-scorched shrubs and trees.

'Do you want the Brits out of here completely?' he asked with a sly smile.

'Sure, I want them out of *everywhere*,' Mairead replied.

Sean pointed up to where the cable car was climbing the cliff face. 'Up there are the Barbary apes. It's said that if the apes ever leave Gibraltar, then the Brits will lose it. So why not, instead of bombing during the ceremony on Tuesday, go up there instead with a couple of sub-machine-guns and blast all the apes to kingdom come. When you've killed the last ape, the Brits will be finished here for good. No apes, no Brits.'

Mairead chuckled. 'Ackaye, it sounds good in theory, but not quite what we're after.'

'So we do it?' Mad Dan asked anxiously. 'We bomb the shites as planned?'

'Aye, I suppose we'll do it,' Mairead told him. 'I have my doubts because of the school and the old people's home, but we've done worse in the past, I suppose. You're right – there are no innocents in war – and we didn't come all this way for nothin'. We have to finish what we started. There's not really a choice now.'

'On Tuesday?' Mad Dan asked, looking relieved.

'Aye, on Tuesday. We'll leave the car we've come in today as a blocker and take a bus back to Marbella. On Tuesday morning, we'll come back here in the bomb-car. At the La Línea gate, Sean will get out of the bomb-car an' walk from there to the blocker in the car park. We'll give him fifteen minutes, then follow him in the bomb-car. At a time to be decided between us, but when the Changin' of the Guard has begun, we'll drive up behind the parked blocker and then Sean, when he sees us right behind him, will drive off and leave us the space. Sean will stop in his car just before leavin' the car park. When we've parked the bomb-car, we'll get out, lock it, and join Sean in the other car. Sean will then drive us back across the airport and back into Spain. The

183

bomb-car will be set to explode about ten minutes after we've exited Gibraltar by the La Línea gate and are well on the way back to Marbella. We should be fairly safe then, and from there we'll drive across Spain to Bilbao. Then we take the boat back to Britain and head on home with no bother.'

'Perfect,' Mad Dan said, pleased at last.

'Aye, right,' Sean said. 'Now let's make our way back to the border.'

They returned to the square forty minutes later, at 3.25, to once again look at the car, checking its position in the crowded car park. Then they turned away, left the car park, and headed north, back to the border.

Sitting in his HQ in the command centre deep within the Rock, Captain Edwards was informed by Mary Hattersley, still out in the streets, of the movements of the three terrorists.

'They're studying the Renault,' she had said over the transceiver. 'There are some kids nearby . . . McCann is looking thoughtfully at the car . . . Now he's speaking to the other two . . . Farrell seems to be amused . . . Now they're all moving off, out of the car park. They have smiles on their faces . . . Yes, definitely: they're leaving the car in the car park and heading back to the border on foot. They've just gone out of sight.'

Learning this, Edwards instantly assumed that the Renault had been left there as a blocker or a bomb-car and that, either way, it and the terrorists themselves had to be dealt with before the latter left the Rock.

'In that case,' said the Police Commissioner, who had been in the crowded command centre since morning and appeared to be excited and nervous at the same time, 'we must formally pass the situation to the Army and let your men get on with it.'

'Good,' Edwards said. 'The other surveillance teams aren't expecting to go into action for another thirty-six hours, but I'm going to deploy them right now, to put a ring of steel around the terrorists. We'll also have that car checked out.'

'Very wise,' the Commissioner said.

While the Commissioner was preparing to sign the relevant documentation, transferring authority for the operation from his own men to the Army, Edwards contacted his two SAS teams to fill them in on the situation.

'Good,' Carruthers replied on hearing that the Army was soon going to be in charge. 'We were beginning to feel a bit hamstrung, waiting for the police to act. This should make it much easier.'

'Exactly,' Edwards said. 'Now keep on the terrorists' tail, don't let them out of your sight, but do nothing until I can confirm that we're formally in charge.'

'Make sure you do it before they cross the border,' Carruthers said. 'And that won't be long, boss.'

'I will, Sarge. Don't worry.'

When Edwards conveyed the same information to his MI5 watchers, they were less enthusiastic about the transfer of authority.

'These last-minute changes aren't helpful,' Hattersley said, 'at such a crucial phase of the operation. They could cause some confusion.'

'There's nothing to be confused about,' Edwards reassured her. 'Very soon we'll be in sole command, and once I've confirmed that, you can move the men in with all possible speed. Meanwhile, please keep me informed of their movements.'

'Will do,' Hattersley said.

'What's happening right now?'

'Team One is following them past the Garrison Theatre and I'm only a short way behind them. Team Two has disappeared up ahead of them, hoping to box the terrorists in.'

'Excellent,' Edwards said. 'Over and out.'

As Edwards cut Hattersley off, he saw that the Commissioner was in heated discussion with someone on the telephone. When the Commissioner had hung up, he turned to face Edwards, mopped sweat from his flushed face with a handkerchief, and said nervously: 'I've changed my mind, Captain. I'm resuming control again. I want another identity check of the three suspects before making any kind of decision regarding what we should do.'

'With all due respect, Commissioner,' Edwards replied, practically grinding his teeth, 'the identity of those three terrorists has already been checked by the security officers at both borders and independently by two MI5 watchers. There's simply no doubt about who they are and . . .'

'We have to be . . .'

'. . . and we have to move in on them before they cross back into Spain. And time's running out, Commissioner.'

The Commissioner kept mopping sweat from his face and glancing anxiously about him, as if looking for help from an invisible ally.

'The car,' he said. 'Perhaps we should at least . . .'

'It's being checked out this very minute by one of the three regular Army officers on my team, a lieutenant from the Royal Army Ordnance Corps.' Edwards checked his watch. 'He should be calling through any second now.'

As the Commissioner was nodding his agreement, a call came through from Hattersley.

'What's happening?' she asked.

'I thought you'd tell *me* that,' Edwards snapped.

'I mean about the transfer of authority. The terrorists are halfway to the border and it's not a long walk. If you want to challenge them, you'll have to do it soon. Time's running out.'

'A slight delay,' Edwards replied, trying to sound calmer than he felt. 'The Commissioner's resumed control for now and is waiting to hear from Lieutenant Raleigh regarding the Renault left in the car park.'

'We haven't time for that, sir.'

'The call should be coming through any second now. I think we . . .' The call was indeed coming through on the receiver held open especially for it. 'That's it,' Edwards said. 'I'll get back to you in a couple of minutes. Over and out.'

Cutting Hattersley off, Edwards picked up the other receiver and said: 'HQ. Flavius. Captain Edwards speaking.'

'Lieutenant Raleigh here, sir. I've visually inspected the white Renault 5 . . .'

'And?' Edwards interjected impatiently.

'I suspect it's a car bomb.'

'Not just a blocker?'

'No.'

'If you've only visually inspected it . . .'

'I'm not allowed to break into it.'

'Fine. If you've only visually inspected it, what makes you think it's the car bomb and not just a blocker?'

'It's a fairly new Renault, but the aerial placed centrally on the roof is old and rusty. That makes me think it may not be the original aerial and therefore that the car's been tampered with.'

'You think the aerial could be part of a remote-control detonator?'

'It's a distinct possibility, Captain.'

187

'Thanks. Over and out.'

Edwards cut Raleigh off and turned back to the sweating Commissioner.

'I heard him,' the Commissioner said.

'So what's your decision, Commissioner? Time's of the essence now.'

'Where are the terrorists right now?'

'Still walking north towards the border. They'll soon be in Winston Churchill Avenue. After that, there's only the runway, then the Spanish border.'

The Commissioner wiped his face yet again and licked his dry lips. 'If you think there's a bomb in that car and sign a declaration saying so, we could arrest all three terrorists on suspicion of conspiracy to murder.'

'I'll sign,' Edwards said.

'No need,' the Commissioner replied with a sheepish grin. 'Just checking. I wanted to be sure you're convinced. All right, let's proceed.' He turned back to the desk behind him, leant over it, withdrew a pen from his breast pocket, and signed the document that had been lying there for hours. When he had signed, he handed a copy to Edwards. 'You're now formally in charge of Operation Flavius,' he informed Edwards. 'The best of luck, Captain.'

Shoving the document carelessly into a pocket in his tunic, the exultant Edwards grabbed the radio microphone and sent out his instructions to all concerned.

'Intercept and apprehend!' he ordered. 'Intercept and apprehend!'

16

Even as Mary Hattersley was whispering into her radio to summon the two SAS CQB teams, the three terrorists were walking through the suburban sprawl where Smith Darrien Road runs into Winston Churchill Avenue, the north-south dual carriageway leading to the runway and, beyond it, the border.

'The parked Renault is believed to be a bomb-car,' Mary whispered into the transceiver. 'Repeat: a bomb-car. The target subjects might therefore be armed and carrying button-jobs. Situation alert. Intercept and apprehend. Intercept and apprehend with caution.'

'Message received,' Sergeant Carruthers of Team Two said. 'Over and out.'

'Message received,' Sergeant Ainsworth of Team One said also. 'Over and out.'

Having converged at Rodney House, at the junction of Smith Darrien Road and Corral Road, both teams conferred urgently before separating once more and moving north again in pursuit of the terrorists.

'If the Renault 5 in the car park *is* a bomb-car, not a blocker,' Carruthers said, 'then either one or all of the terrorists will be carrying a button-job and all of them are almost certainly armed. That means we have to approach them with caution – and I mean *extreme* caution. We have to formally challenge them, but be prepared to fire if they make any quick move that suggests they're either going to detonate the bomb or withdraw their weapons. The aim is to intercept and apprehend, but we have to be prepared to neutralize them with all possible speed. OK, let's go.'

Shortly after entering Winston Churchill Avenue, when they were at the petrol station opposite the six-storey Lugana Estate apartment complex, the terrorists stopped and started talking to one another. As they were talking, both SAS teams took up positions on the same side of the avenue, but some yards south, spaced well apart and loitering like ordinary citizens. Though they could clearly see the terrorists, they couldn't hear what they were saying, but assumed that they had stopped merely for a rest and a chat in the sun.

'What's the problem?' Sean asked.

'I've just had a thought,' Mairead replied. 'I think we're makin' a mistake here. As I said before, we might be under surveillance an' if we are then they'll know that parked car's ours. Also, if they checked us as we came across the border, they'll know that Sean drove in an' we . . .' – she nodded to indicate Mad Dan – 'came in together on foot a couple of hours later. They might be wonderin', then, about why we're all leavin' together an' put two and two together the wrong way, mistakin' that blocker for a bomb-car. If they do, either they'll close the car park for a demolitions search of the blocker or they'll arrest us at the border as we try to cross back into Spain.'

'Aye, you're right there,' Mad Dan conceded. 'So what should we do?'

'I think we should leave the way we came in,' Mairead told him. 'You and me together on foot; Sean travelling separately in the car. Then, to be sure, once back in Marbella we change the car for another – not a Renault 5 – and bring it back late tomorrow afternoon and park it as another blocker. Also, that way, the blocker will only be in the car park for one night and part of the mornin' before we explode the bomb. What do you think?'

'I agree,' Sean said.

'Aye, me too,' Mad Dan agreed.

'Right, Sean, you get goin',' Mairead said, 'back to the car park. Meanwhile, me and Dan'll go on and cross into Spain. You can pick us up at the bar we were in before, just beyond the La Línea gate, and the three of us can then drive back to Marbella as planned previously.'

'Right,' Sean said, turning immediately and walking back the way the three of them had come, towards the centre of town, while Mairead and Mad Dan started away from the petrol station, again intending to head north towards the border.

As Sean moved away from the other two, Ainsworth and Billings moved out from the side to the centre of the pavement. Unconcerned, Sean kept walking towards them, then skirted around the sergeant, his shoulder lightly bumping him as he passed.

Ainsworth had been fully prepared to shout the challenge and then summon the police by radio while covering the three terrorists with his drawn Browning. Now, however, with the group breaking up to go in two directions, one of them actually brushing past him, he experienced a momentary confusion that threw him off balance.

He's going to detonate the bomb-car, he thought as the terrorist passed him and headed on down the avenue.

When Ainsworth jerked around, however, starting to reach behind him for his handgun, he first caught a glimpse of Billings's equally confused face, then saw that Carruthers and Dymock had stepped out of the side of the pavement and were already hurrying down the avenue to catch up with Savage.

'Go after McCann and Farrell,' he heard the voice of Carruthers saying tinnily in his covert microphone. 'Intercept and apprehend.'

'Let's go,' Ainsworth said to Billings, knowing he had also heard the instruction. '*Now*!'

Never a gentleman, Mad Dan was walking along the inside of the pavement, away from the road, close to the low wall flanking the petrol station. Mairead walked on his left, nearer the gutter, frequently brushing her hair away from her eyes when the wind made it whip around her pale, haunted face.

Suddenly, as if by instinct, Mad Dan looked back over his shoulder – directly at the two SAS men. He was smiling.

That smile on the lips of a man known to have killed many people and reported to be mad sent a chill combination of fear and revulsion through Ainsworth.

Mad Dan's wild eyes fixed him. They looked directly at each other. Then, as if his killer's instincts had told him that something was wrong – that these two men coming up behind him were not ordinary civilians – Mad Dan stopped smiling and stiffened into animal alertness.

Reacting instinctively, Ainsworth went for his Browning. As he did so, Mad Dan's right arm moved across the front of his body and the SAS man, thinking he was going for the button-job, about to detonate the bomb, dropped into the 'double tap' firing position and took aim, holding the pistol in both hands.

The weapon was already loaded. One round was in the breech and the firing pin was cocked. A quick flick of the thumb released the safety-catch and then Ainsworth squeezed the trigger.

The first round went into Mad Dan's back as his arm was still moving across the front of his body. He jerked violently, flung his hands above his shoulders, then staggered drunkenly sideways, already collapsing.

As the sound of the shot rang out, probably even before she had seen that Mad Dan was hit, Mairead grabbed for the bag under her arm. Assuming that she was reaching for a button control or weapon, Ainsworth aimed at her and fired. He kept firing at the rate of one shot approximately every second and a half, turning the Browning on Mad Dan a second time as he continued firing.

Even before Mad Dan had fallen to the ground, he took one shot to the body and two to the head, with his skull smashed open.

A police siren wailed.

Hearing it, Ainsworth raised both hands, still gripping the pistol, and shouted: 'Police!'

Hearing that single, bawled word, Billings also opened fire, putting seven bullets into Mairead and Mad Dan even as they were falling.

As Mairead twisted to the ground with blood pouring from her face and back, Billings shot her again because he could not see her hands and feared she still might press the button control. Only when she had flopped on to the pavement with her hands away from her body – thus away from a weapon or the button control – did Billings ease his finger off the trigger.

Behind Ainsworth and Billings, Hattersley, at the sound of the first shot, had already called up one of the police cars that had been following the hunted and the hunters alike from a discreet distance. This accounted for the siren that had been heard in the distance and was growing rapidly louder as the car approached the killing ground.

Seeing no movement from either terrorist, Ainsworth, covered carefully by Billings, the latter still aiming his Browning in the two-handed position, ran forward and knelt down to examine the two motionless terrorists. The woman, he saw immediately, had been shot four times in the face and also in the back, with blood spreading out from under her, all around her. Both terrorists were dead.

'Good riddance,' Ainsworth murmured as he straightened up, gave the 'All clear' signal to Billings, and waited for the police car.

Within seconds, the car had pulled up to spirit the two SAS men away from the scene of the shooting.

As the first bullets were hitting the two terrorists, Sean Savage was 120 yards away, walking in the opposite direction, along Corral Road, towards the Landport Gate. He was unaware that he was being tailed by Carruthers and Dymock, who in turn were being followed by the other MI5 watcher, Barbara Jennings.

When Sean heard the shooting and the police siren, he spun around and saw the two men following him. They raced up to him, guns already drawn as part of the intercept-and-apprehend SOP.

'Stop!' Carruthers bawled. 'Police! Get down! Hands above your head! Stay still!'

Shocked, Sean ignored the bawled instructions and instead reached down instinctively to his jacket pocket, forgetting that he did not have a pistol and dropping into the CQB stance that he had learnt with the IRA. Seeing that move-ment, Carruthers didn't think twice about opening fire.

Only fifteen yards away, Jennings turned her head aside, not wanting to see the rest of what was happening. She heard a wailing police siren, a buzzing from her earpiece, and, above the buzzing, more gunshots. Nevertheless, she managed to put through a call for another police car.

Carruthers carried on firing as the terrorists's body spiralled down, hitting him four times in the chest and twice in the head. At the same time, a woman walking towards the Landport Gate accidentally got between Dymock and the falling terrorist. With his free arm, Dymock pushed the woman aside, then, with his other hand, drew his pistol and fired nine shots.

He fired the first round and carried on firing, very rapidly, into Sean's body as the terrorist was shuddering violently and falling away to the ground. The last two rounds were aimed at his head when it was mere inches away from the ground, just before his skull cracked against the pavement and his body went limp.

Dymock kept on firing until the terrorist was absolutely still and his hands were well away from his body. Then, as Dymock kept Carruthers covered, the latter ran forward and checked that the IRA man was well and truly dead. Seeing that his body was riddled with bullets, his head had been virtually pulverized, and he appeared to be losing blood from every pore, Carruthers knew that he was dead.

Within seconds, a second wailing police car stopped by the two SAS men and they jumped into the back and were driven away.

Ten minutes later all four SAS men handed their weapons and unused ammunition to the Gibraltar police, then went to report to Edwards, who congratulated them on a job well done and reassured them that if the killings were queried, he would stand strongly behind them.

'Not that there *will* be queries,' he added. 'Clearly you did what you had to do.'

In fact, before being flown back to England the two SAS teams learnt that no bomb had been found in the Renault and that none of the terrorists had been armed.

Postscript

Operation Flavius became the most contentious in the history of the SAS, with the men involved being described as an officially sanctioned 'special assassination squad' and 'an unholy priesthood of violence'. The outrage was only compounded by the fact that the terrorists had not been armed and no bomb was found in the parked Renault 5. And nor was the SAS helped by the fact that many of the official watchers professed to have seen nothing while civilian witnesses not only came forward with detailed statements but, in more than one instance, insisted that the SAS had shot their victims without provocation and in the back while they were unaware or while they were spread out on the ground.

Mairead Farrell had been shot four times in the face and three times in the back, dying of two wounds in the heart and one in the liver, though other bullets had also broken her back. At least sixteen bullets had been shot into Sean Savage and he had suffered a total of twenty-nine injuries, including those shot into his head from above, either just before he hit the ground or as he actually lay on it. Daniel McCann had been hit by a similar number of bullets, both front and rear.

At the inquest conducted in September 1988 the four SAS troopers defended the killings by saying that although they had been given orders to arrest the terrorists, they were also given permission to use their weapons 'if those using them had reasonable grounds for believing that an act was being committed or about to be committed which would endanger life or lives and if there was no other way of preventing that other than with firearms'.

Certain Spanish officials expressed a sense of betrayal at the killing of the terrorists. One claimed that the British informed him that the terrorists had died in a 'shoot-out', which clearly was not true. The same official complained that by killing all the terrorists, instead of only one or two, the SAS had left the Spanish authorities in the uncomfortable position of having no one to question regarding the location of the car bomb.

However, the notion that the Spanish police may not have been informed about the anti-terrorist operation, may have been misinformed, and may have been seriously outraged by it was placed in serious doubt when, in March the following year, twenty-two Spanish police officers received citations for their part in the surveillance operation preceding the killings.

The death of the three terrorists resulted in questions being asked about the amount of control exercised over the SAS, about whether or not they had a licence to kill, and about whether or not the British government, specifically Prime Minister Margaret Thatcher, had ordered them to kill the terrorists rather than capture them.

The debate raged throughout the following months and was not extinguished by the inquest's verdict in September 1988 that the three had been lawfully killed.

The SAS were vindicated somewhat by the official announcement that the Spanish police had found the IRA's car bomb in an underground car park in Marbella, a location only thirty miles from Gibraltar and one which the terrorists would have had to pass through *en route* to the Rock. The car bomb contained 143lb of Semtex explosive and an unattached timing device set for 1120 hours, which is exactly when the Changing of the Guard ceremony on Gibraltar took place.

The implication, therefore, is that the white Renault 5 parked near the assembly point on Gibraltar on 6 March was indeed a 'blocker' and that the original estimate of a bombing planned for 8 March was correct.

Nevertheless, while this news raised the possibility that the terrorists intended leaving the 'blocker' in the car park in Gibraltar until they returned on 8 March with the bomb-car, there are those who still insist that the car bomb found in the car park in Marbella was a fiction created by the Spanish and British authorities to save them embarrassment.

The truth may never be known.

Though the operation resulted in the 'neutralization' of a highly dangerous IRA Active Service Unit, whether intended or not, the publicity surrounding the affair was deemed negative from the Regiment's point of view as it prefers to work covertly, well away from the attention of the media.

In June 1994 the European Commission of Human Rights decided that the SAS soldiers involved in the Gibraltar killings did not use unnecessary force in violation of the European human rights conventions. Eleven members of the Commission found in favour of the British government, but six dissented. At the time of writing, the European Court of Human Rights has yet to make its final decision regarding the matter.